THE PARTING GLASS

THE PARTING GLASS

Michael O'Grady

Acc. No. 18/3756

Class No. F

No. 14659

Copyright © Michael O' Grady 2011

ISBN 978-1-907107-69-6

First Published 2011 in cooperation with
Choice Publishing, Drogheda, Co Louth
www.choicepublishing.ie

Editing: John Prendergast

All rights reserved. No part of this publication may be reproduced, stored in or introduced into a retrieval system, or transmitted, in any form, or by any means (electronic, mechanical, photocopying, recording or otherwise) without the prior written permission of the publisher. Any person who does any unauthorised act in relation to this publication may be liable to criminal prosecution and civil claims for damages.

The characters in this book are purely fictional. Any similarities between them and real individuals are purely coincidental.

For Bernie
Who taught me how to live and love again
And for my adorable children

1.

Good news or bad news can help to break the monotony in a nine-to-five job. On this particular day in November, there was not such good news for one Thomas Meade. It appeared that while singing a charming ditty with the fullness of voice, Thomas's mind was not on his job – which was sawing a piece of plywood – but on the tune itself. Two of his unfortunate fingers met with the tungsten tipped blade and were severed into a pit of shavings some twenty feet away beside the four-cutter. The singing stopped instantly and was replaced by a ferocious outburst of pain. All of the twenty-two employees in the joinery shop ran to the rescue. Within seconds an ambulance was called, and soon afterwards Thomas was escorted to the Adelaide Hospital.

Albert Cagney sat in shock, gazing out through the plate-glass window of the office which faced out into the joinery works.

'Tommy will have to do without his porter tonight,' said Eamonn Coyle, the man sitting next to Albert. 'Are you going for one, Albert?'

It was three years since Albert joined McEwan's and as many more since Eamonn did. Now, Mr Morris Broderick, the man in charge, entered the office door and began conversing with Eamonn about the accident. Albert priced out invoices, trying to look as busy as was possible until the siren sounded dutifully. It was five thirty.

'The end of another day!' Mr. Broderick muttered.

'Thanks be to God,' said Eamonn.

Morris Broderick coughed his way out of the office.

*

Kenny's Public House was at the corner of Bride Street, not a stone's throw away form the Ivy Hostel. With its concrete floors and hard wooden seats the pub usually only enticed a clientele from the working classes. Albert procured two seats while Eamonn went to get two pints of plain porter. They were immediately joined by some of their fellow employees, both male and female, and soon the bar was full. It was Friday evening and everyone had just been paid; now they conversed over the injustices bestowed upon them by their employers over the past week. Intermingled in these conversations every three words or so were Anglo-Saxon four letter words, or else words pertaining to a certain part of the male anatomy.

'Get that into you, Albert,' Eamonn said as he returned with the drinks. 'I'm not talking to you Sandra! That'll be later.'

Eamonn started talking to the girls from the office and Albert watched as they sat prey to all of Eamonn's charms. Albert looked on him as a person of remarkable vigour. Eamonn was some four years his senior, being all of twenty-three, and in contrast to Albert, he was dark skinned and ruggedly handsome.

Tony Royal sat down beside them. He was a labourer, about twenty-five, who had spent his last day working for McEwan's and was about to embark on a career in the army. He bought more drinks than could possibly be needed for human consumption. Time passed and Albert felt drunk. The bar had become crowded with people and smoke. It became increasingly noisy. A free-for-all broke out in the far corner between some middle-aged people.

'Listen lads', said Albert. 'I have to go.'

'I'm off myself,' Eamonn agreed as he stood up.

'I'll walk a bit of the way with you,' said Tony to Albert. 'I know where we can get something nice to eat!'

Albert bid farewell to Eamonn with the daunting assurance that the next time they would meet would be for their arduous labours on Monday. Then he and Tony walked out into the mild November evening.

'Let's walk up to Burdocks!' Tony said. 'We'll get nice fish and chips there, then we'll cut back through Ship Street and be on the Green in a minute. Come on, Albert. Let's make a night of it.'

Albert had wanted to be alone, but he enjoyed the company of Tony; and besides, he felt obliged to stay with him on account of it being their last day working together.

*

Albert originally came from the outskirts of Limerick, but now he lived in a flat on Leeson Street. It was a new abode for him, and this was his first week there. The flat was on a top floor of a four-story building. Archaic, almost derelict, with a large damp gable wall: it was an impressive big double room with a bed, four chairs and a table, facing a mass of equally tall Georgian buildings, and was just five minutes from Stephen's Green and O' Dwyer's and Hannigan's public houses. The Focus Theatre and the Pembroke Bar were around the corner in Pembroke Street.

Albert opened the door as gracefully as he could, and tiptoed his way up the stairs, beckoning his friend to follow. He had his index finger placed upright across his mouth and was gently saying 'hush' as they wended their way upwards towards his room.

'I wouldn't like the landlord to catch me with drink on me the first week in his flat,' Albert whispered.

3

'Fuck him, aren't you paying him enough for it? This is a fantastic place, and it's right where the brassers are! Did you ever go over and pick one up?'

'Brassers?' said Albert.

'Surely you know what a brasser is! A prostitute. Don't tell me you're still a virgin – that you never got it yet? What age are you now?'

A delicate shade of puce formed on Albert's face. 'I'm nineteen and I didn't.'

'Here, get a cup of tea, it'll make you feel better. And then we'll go down and get a few more pints. Come on! Let's make a night of it.'

*

Albert sat beside the door in Hannigan's in an effort to catch as much air as possible. He observed a tall gracious lady standing at the bar. She had roaring red hair, freckles and a long black dress, and spoke with the authority of a university lecturer to an elderly gentleman whom Albert thought to be an actor he had seen on stage.

'Do you feel alright?' Tony said. 'You look a bit lost there. Do you know that bird?

'No,' said Albert.

'We'll finish up these few pints, and saunter up to the Pepper Canister and have a good time.'

Although illegal, this was the red light district in Dublin. Albert was unaware of this fact, but for the pleasure of obtaining fresh air he was prepared to go anywhere.

*

Rousing ballads and come-all-yous were common occurrences

amongst Dublin folk – especially when they had imbibed more than their fair share of alcohol. For Albert and Tony it was no different, as they staggered up Leeson Street towards the Pepper Canister singing to their hearts content.

'Stop!' ordered Tony. 'Look, she's a peach!'

Not thirty feet away, standing by a railing surrounding a small park were some women talking to each other. The occasional car pulled in, the driver chatting for an instant, then driving away.

'They must be asking too much,' said Tony. 'Let's go around by Fitzwilliam Place.'

Albert was flabbergasted to see that it was true; these girls were actually of easy virtue. Stirred and shaken, he continued on around the park. Standing next to a willow tree was a tall long-legged lady. She wore a plastic see-through mackintosh which underneath revealed an extremely short mini-skirt.

'Come on,' said Tony. 'She's a fucking doll! Let's see what's the story here.'

Albert's heart beat at a rapid rate. He could feel his knees beginning to wobble.

'I'll stay h-here, Tony. You go ahead.' He coughed to hide the tremble in his voice.

Tony walked towards the young lady while Albert looked on. They talked for a while; to Albert it seemed an age. There was the occasional twitter of laughter from both, and Albert wondered if Tony had told the girl about him; about the fact that he was a virgin. Maybe they were laughing at his expense. A slight drizzle of rain had started. Albert fretted and grew damp until Tony returned.

'She's a peach, but she's asking three pounds. Let's go bleeding home. I'm bollixed. I couldn't afford that.'

They passed by her and Tony bid her good night. Albert caught a sidelong glimpse of her beautiful figure and her classically chiselled face. He was speechless.

5

At Leeson Street they talked for a time until Tony hailed a taxi. 'Here Albert, take care of yourself. I'll give you a shout in a couple of weeks.'

Albert bid him farewell, and stood leaning against the wall to give his breathing a chance to return to normal. Cars streamed busily up and down Leeson Street and the rain had become heavier. Should he return to Fitzwilliam Place? Perhaps she would be soaked to the skin and he could offer her shelter? Or was it something else that attracted his mind to her? Was he fooling himself, being so enamoured? He had to meet her and go the whole way. He shivered, and his heart hammered inside his chest.

Turning back, he walked briskly. His mind was wandering again. Maybe Tony did tell her he was a virgin? Perhaps she would laugh at him. Perhaps she noticed that twitch of nervousness in his face as they had passed.

She still stood by the tree as he approached. He took a deep breath and walked towards her.

'Are you alright love?' she said. 'Can I do anything for you? You look drenched.'

'H-how much are you asking?' asked Albert, trembling.

'That depends on what you want, love. Have you a car?'

'No, I haven't. But I have a flat in Leeson Street?'

'You want the VIP treatment. We'd want to get to know you first. Are you a TD's son? Ah no, love. We don't go into men's flats.'

Her voice was English, soft and sweet. He could not take his eyes away from her. He pointed towards the gates of the park, inside of which were six-foot bushes. 'C-could we d-do it in there, Miss?'

She gave a pleasant smile, which eased the tension of his situation. 'You're new around here. You're not one of the regulars?'

'No. I've never been here before.'

'You have an honest-looking face. I suppose rules are made to be broken. Okay love. Do you live far from here? It'll cost you three quid. My name's Jill. What's yours?'

'Albert. Albert Cagney.'

'Nothing to James?' She laughed.

Albert moved swiftly down Leeson Street while Jill lagged behind. The danger of the landlord seeing him with drink on him was now replaced by the possibility of being found in the company of this girl. When they reached the flat, Albert noticed a light on over the black hall door. He whispered to Jill that he lived on the top floor and they moved briskly up the stairs.

'This place is creepy. Did they film the werewolf films here?'

'I only moved in the other day.'

'I'm only joking you. It's a big room. Shall we get down to business? Have you three quid?'

Albert fumbled in his pocket, and took out five pounds.

'Have you any change, Miss? I mean Jill, isn't it?'

'Jill is right, love. For five you can have a really good time.'

'You can keep it.'

Jill began to undress, while Albert turned away towards the moonlit window. His heart was pounding as he gazed down to the street; and so were his pants. A drunk sat on the sidewalk holding a bottle of wine and muttering to himself. A policeman approached and urged him to move on. In the glass, Albert faced his reflection: though he was tall, nineteen years of age and athletically built, he had a pale complexion, with blond hair and blue eyes. Amongst his friends he was no Greek Adonis. But, by the same token, they would not have given vent to the expression, 'he has a face like the back of a bus'.

'Aren't you going to get ready, love? It seems pointless getting undressed alone.'

Albert turned around; Jill stood naked in front of him. He was speechless. The blood seemed to have left his body. He was sure his circulation had stopped. His face grew paler and he felt his head had locked and his heart was missing beats.

She was beautiful, more beautiful than he could ever have imagined. Why had he met her the way that he did? This was surely the girl of his dreams. He was nervous, felt cheap, small, and was shaking; he had paid her for this. The sight of her nakedness sobered him completely. He wished it was a lion that stood in front of him for he would be better able to cope. He felt sorry that they had not met before under different circumstances.

'Are you alright, love? You're not having a bleedin' stroke? We're not insured for the likes of death. Like, "found dead on the job". Do you know what I mean? Are you after having a mild heart attack?'

'I'm okay, but you... I can't go through with it. You can put your clothes back on.'

'There's no refund, love, when you order from the menu. Once the proper lunch is put in front of you, it's up to you whether you want to eat or not.' Jill began to dress. 'I'd like a cup of tea, if you have any.'

'Yes! I have,' Albert said, taking hold of his senses.

Jill sat by the fire, and when the tea was ready Albert sat opposite her. He looked up towards her face and saw her eyes were a delicate shade of blue. Jill looked at him and smiled, revealing her pearl-white teeth and pale, pink lips. Her dark eyebrows were perfect, not a hair out of place, and her long blonde hair hung down to her half-covered, firm round breasts.

'You haven't been around the town much, have you?'

'No'

'It's a strange business. I've met all sorts, but you're a strange one.'

'What brought you into this?'

'You mean as low as this. Some other time, love. It's a long story. No, it's not a long story; it's a short story. It just takes a long time to tell it.'

She got up to leave.

Albert walked her down to the door, and when they got there she stopped.

'Look, I'm sorry…Albert, isn't it? Would you take even a kiss?'

Albert nodded uncomfortably.

She pressed her soft lips gently against his and put her arms fondly around his waist, giving him a warm embrace. As she moved away, she stopped and paused for an instant, looking at him. 'Bye. Another time perhaps.' Jill turned and walked across the street.

She had not gone more than fifty yards when Albert ran after her in a state of panic.

'I know this is strange,' he said, 'but… could I see you again? I mean, I don't mean as a-a you-know-what, but… as a friend. You see, I only moved in around here the other day, and I don't know friends from here.'

'Are you soft in the head? You don't even know me.'

'Isn't that the same with everyone before they go on a date?'

'I'll be in the Pembroke bar tomorrow. I might see you there at eight.'

'Thanks.'

Jill smiled as she stopped a taxi. Albert watched as the car headed towards Stephen's Green.

*

He felt warm with joy as he lay in bed. All sleep abandoned him. Through the sash of the window, grey black clouds drifted overhead. Could this be a new beginning? With this thought, he fell asleep. It was three-thirty a.m.

2.

'I wasn't going to turn up, I'll have you know. I just felt a bit sorry for you, that's all. You know, we get asked out on dates all the time by clients. You might look at us, and ask what kind of girls are we? But we look at fellows, and ask what kind of fellows pick up us kind of girls?'

Albert noticed that her English accent had disappeared.

Jill sat beside Albert, who was sitting on a high stool by the bar. 'You had a good few jars on you last night,' she said. 'You're not one of those fellows really, are you? I'm going to an audition, they're looking for a model. Are you here long?'

'Not long. You're all wound up. It's great to hear you're taking up modelling, I'd say you'd be good at it. What would you like to drink?'

'Vodka, with a splash of red.'

'Would you like to see a play in the Gate theatre? It's called Lady Windermere's Fan?'

'Let's get a drink first.'

Walking up the stairs of the Gate theatre held a certain magic for Albert. It was the theatrical atmosphere that surrounded it; the carpets, the curtains the cornice, the paintings, the pictures, the people, the odour, and now most importantly, his lady friend at his side. Jill held his hand as they passed the coffee foyer. They looked at pictures and contemplated photos of past productions and players before taking their seats for the play to commence.

Jill removed her coat. She wore pink high-heeled shoes and a white satin blouse which hung halfway down her pink leather mini-skirt.

Albert, using only the orbs of his eyes for fear she might notice, peered slowly from her shoes along her shapely legs. 'Are you comfortable?' he asked.

'Yes! And I'm looking forward to it' She pressed his hand tightly as they turned and faced the curtain.

How happy he was, yet also a little uneasy. What would he say were she bored? Where would he take her afterwards? The audience coughed, whispered and turned pages in their programmes until their attention was caught by the diming of the lights and the opening of the curtain. Theatre had been the dominant passion in Albert's life since his early days, along with admiring nature and exploring the mountains in Wicklow. He had spent endless hours at a local picture house, marvelling at the acting of Brando, Cagney, Bogart and the like. Often he would ramble through from Joyce to Beckett land on day outings, from Anna Liffey to Sandymount, or for a refreshing contrast spend his time amongst the Wicklow hills. Now, as always when the show began, his spirit left his body to encircle the stage, engrossed in sheer fantasy with the players.

*

11

They proceeded to the coffee foyer during the interval.

'Will you have something to drink, tea or orange? They don't sell anything stronger, here.'

'It's a smoke I really want,' Jill said. 'Would you like one of these?' She offered him a cigarette from the packet.

'Okay. I'll just get two oranges. What do you think of the play?'

'They're very posh and all that, aren't they? I feel bleedin' weird. Like I NEVER saw that kind of thing before. I come from the flats. What are you staring at me like that for? Like I was a prize cow up for sale?'

'I'm sorry, I was just noticing how pretty you look.'

'Ah! Give over, for fuck's sake.'

A rather obese looking gentleman overheard their idle talk, and gave a disgruntled cough at the idea of such a conversation in, above all places, the theatre.

*

When the play was over, they walked the whole way to Leeson Street, talking and joking freely. Albert turned on the electric fire, and was making his way towards the sink to put water in the kettle.

'Here I'll do that,' Jill said.

They sat on the two fireside chairs, facing each other, drinking tea.

'It's a pity we never met before,' she said. 'We may have something special between us. Things might have been different. What I'm saying is… I wish you'd have known me, before you knew about me. You know. The way we met and all that. There's a more serious side to me. You're a nice guy.'

There was a quiver in Jill's voice, and her watery eyes belied her forced smile.

'Don't worry about it, Jill. We met now, didn't we?' He slipped down on his knees and put his arm around her neck, bringing his lips towards hers. They kissed.

Albert knew what she was talking about. He was curious about how one so beautiful had chosen such a precarious profession; he desperately wanted to know why, but was afraid he might hear something that might mar the magic of their embrace. Jill was right. It might haunt him for the rest of the time he would know her.

Without thinking, he surprised himself by asking, 'Why don't you tell me about it?'

'I'm sorry, Albert, not now. I had a great evening.' Jill stood up and walked gracefully towards the door.

Albert walked her down the long stairway to the street. 'I'll walk you home.'

'That's alright, I'm used to it.' She smiled.

'I'd like to.'

*

They walked out into the dark night. They said nothing, but multitudes of thoughts passed in the silences. He held her hand like a father with a lost child as they made their way up Camden Street.

'Can I see you Saturday?'

'If you want to.'

'I'll see you in the Pembroke again then,' he said.

They kissed.

*

It was two in the morning when he got to bed. He laid his head on the pillow. The moon shone through his room from the three-by-two foot sash window. What a strange girl, he thought. He wanted to know more about her; yet he was afraid that if he got too involved it would only break both their hearts. His mind turned over the fearful thought until he fell asleep.

Peader sat on a bench in a hut behind the panel planer. Some of the employees used this as a canteen. He was seventy years of age, but held in his looks everybody's version of the perfect grandad. Albert was reading a book, while his friend and co-worker Skipper stood reading The Mirror.

Another colleague, Tim, walked in to join them. 'You're a terrible man Skipper, and you married. What do you think of that, Peader?'

'What ails him now?' said Peader, taking a puff on his pipe.

'A different one last night. I saw him walking up the Rathmines Road. She was mighty, all of fourteen stone.'

'Isn't that the way to have them!' Skipper said. 'Big and round to go around. I'll let them know I'm around!'

'You ought to be ashamed of yourself, and you married,' Peader said. 'You'll burn in hell!'

'Sure you have to have some fun. They make you appreciate your own. A big broad one from Monaghan, she was. All I did was take her for a walk up the Pine Valley to the fields, and recite her some poetry. Yeats, Shelley, Longfella.'

'You're a blackguard, with no respect for man or beast,' said Peader. 'Sure no bird would be interested in that rubbish.'

'She liked the Longfella! Strange, isn't it? They all seem to like the Longfella!'

There was a general twitter of laughter, more from the smile on Peader's face than the frolics that came from Skipper.

Skipper's proper name was Christy McCabe, but he had acquired the nickname some years previously. He was thirty years of age, with dark hair and a bronze complexion. He had wrinkles in the right places to enhance his masculine features. Like Albert, he was more than a fair amateur actor and he had a passion for the mountain countryside where they spent most weekends.

Tommy, the foreman, was making his way up the yard towards them.

'Jaysis! Here he is, we better get a move on,' Skipper said.

'You weren't here on Friday?' said Albert.

'I took one of my days' holidays. We went climbing in Glendalough. You missed a great weekend. Davey was looking for you.'

'Listen, I've got to talk to you. It's important. I have a problem. I want your advice on something, Skipper.'

'We'll have a pint in the Chinaman after work. Anyway, Davey said he would see you there.' Skipper walked towards the foreman to receive his daily chores.

The day passed like a week for Albert. All his office duties seemed an endless task for his mind was elsewhere. When the five-thirty siren came, he felt like a prisoner reprieved.

*

'We're being sent down to Bond Road tomorrow,' Albert told Skipper as they walked down Chancery Lane towards the Chinaman Public House. 'There's yourself, Peader, Johnny and Tim. Apparently there's a cargo due in.'

'I have to draw water. Call two pints.'

Albert sat at the far corner of the bar. The Chinaman was a favourite haunt of theirs, especially as they served soup and sandwiches during lunch.

'What's all the panic about?' asked Skipper on his return.

16

'It's really personal. You'll have to promise me you'll keep it to yourself.'

'God's truth, I will. You're not in some sort of trouble, are you?'

'I'm in a bit of a mess, and I can't get it out of my head.'

'What's it all about?'

'Well, you see, last Friday, Eamonn, Tony and myself went for a few pints after work. Afterwards, Tony took me up to the Pepper Canister and I met this girl.'

'You haven't a dose of the fucking crabs, have you?'

'It's not like that! No I haven't!'

'Did you check?'

'No! Look, I brought her back to my flat.'

'You were a model, fair play to you. Go on.'

'Will you listen to me? It's not like that. I didn't do anything. We just talked. I took her to a play.'

'Don't tell me; you discovered you're a pigs ear, a queer. Go on with the play?'

'It was Lady Winder—'

'Not that play, the play with your woman.'

'Cut out the messing. I'm no queer. You see, I'm after getting tied up with her and I can't get her out of my mind. But I have to break it off.'

'Why?'

'I'm mad about her, but I know it would eventually break my heart knowing what she was like. I mean – on the game.'

'Are you fucking mad? That's the sort of mot I'm looking for for years! Think of all her mates! You know the old saying; show me your company, and I'll show you what you are. There's hours of fun there. I'll get to know them with you, and we'll have loads of craic.'

'I'm serious; I don't know what to tell her. I mean she's really a nice girl.'

'Nice? She's fucking powerful!'

'She was nearly crying. And she said she wished we'd met before we did. We may have had something between us.'

'You fucking idiot! Why didn't you let her know what you had between you?'

'I'm bringing her to the Pembroke bar on Saturday.'

Their conversation was interrupted by Davey Amstrong. He was nineteen and tall like Albert, with dark mousey hair and soft brown eyes. They had met and become friends on their holidays in Cahirsiveen at the age of thirteen.

'You didn't go to the hills last Saturday?'

'I'm sorry Davey, moving and that, I didn't get a chance to call and tell you. I'll go Saturday week.'

'Are you having a pint?' Skipper asked.

'I'll get it myself. I'm only having one.'

With Davey gone to the bar, Albert whispered to Skipper not to mention anything about his encounter with the lady. Davey quickly returned.

'I'm doing this course in the Brendan Smith Academy,' said Albert. 'It's starting on Tuesday. It's a course on acting and stagecraft. Anyone interested in joining with me?'

'No fucking way!' said Davey. 'I thought I'd never reach fourteen to get out of school'.

'I'll go along with you,' said Skipper. 'How much does it cost?'

'It's ten quid.'

When they finished their drinks and made their plans, they parted company.

4.

Albert sat in the back row and Skipper secured the seat next to him. It was the first night of the course and Miss Williams was conducting nervous pupils on Voice Production. Albert liked the elderly lady; she seemed ordinary, with no airs or graces.

'And in our sounds,' she said, 'we must have purity, audibility, power to carry and correctness in flowing quality. And this is what we must hear – in our vowel sounds.'

From beside Albert came an unmerciful breaking of wind. It commanded an embarrassing pause from the students.

'Ah! For Jaysis' sake, Albert!' whispered Skipper loudly. 'Take control of yourself!'

Albert felt as though a bomb had dropped in the class. All eyes were focused on him, the supposed guilty party. The blood rushed to his face, and the more he tried to control it the quicker it ran.

'Are you there, Albert?' Skipper whispered. 'Or is that a 6lb tomato I see perched on the shoulder beside me with a wig on top?'

Albert wished the ground would open and swallow him.

'I'm sorry, son. You see I didn't think she said vowel sounds. I thought she said bowel sounds.'

By the end of the night, Albert decided to continue the course. He was fascinated by the thought that this lady could improve his English and teach him to speak correctly. He, like his friend Davey, had left school at fourteen. Skipper, on the other hand, decided he knew more about acting than his tutors. He planned to start by directing a play.

*

Normally Albert sat in his flat each night, reading as much as possible. Poetry and prose, plays and pictures were all magnets to him. With Skipper and Clive, he had spent many hours discussing subjects such as these, often with tears of laughter and delight at thinking something new. He also had a penchant for books on exploration. Davey and himself dreamed of exploring mountains in Ireland, Scotland and even the Alps. Reading about people who measured their strength against the mountains quickened Albert's blood. With Davey, he would marvel at some heroic passage over and over again.

But now all these follies were blurred for him. All his mind could focus on was Jill. The more the week went on, the more he looked forward to their meeting on Saturday night.

5

They sat at a back dim corner of the Pembroke Lounge and were engrossed in conversation when they heard a voice.

'As I live and breath. Fancy meeting you here. A small world, isn't it? You never told me you had a girlfriend, Albert.' Skipper sat down next to them.

Jill extended her hand. 'My name's Jill.'

'Christy McCabe miss, a great friend of Albert. Hold on, I'll get yous a gargle. Do you mind if I join you? That's gas now and I on my Sweeney. What'll it be?'

'I don't want anything,' said Albert. 'We're going shortly.'

'Nor I, thanks a lot,' said Jill.

'Oh I'm very sorry,' said Skipper. 'I'm after intruding in your company. I wasn't trying to be anything but friendly. You see I just saw you with the corner of my eye.'

Jill smiled. 'That's alright. You're welcome to join us. I'll have vodka and a splash of red.'

Skipper left to go to the bar.

'What's the matter, Albert?' said Jill. 'You haven't said a word?'

'He works with me. I don't like meeting people I work with in a pub. I see enough of them all day.'

Skipper could not be trusted; more than that, now he hated him. How could he be so cruel? He should have confided his secret to Eamonn. This was going to be an evening of torture. He looked up through the crowded bar and Skipper caught Albert's eye. With a

21

cunning smile, he gave an upright arm salute through his drunkenness.

He staggered towards them with the drinks. 'Hey Albert, don't think I'm trying to eye up your bit of skirt. I'm married with six kids, Miss, so you can keep your lustful eyes off me. I'm only having the craic. Amn't I, Albert?'

Nothing Skipper could say now could have hurt more. Albert was dazed, mystified, in an unreal vacuum of hate and sorrow. He felt the kind of terror in his mind murderers must feel before they embark on their dreaded deed. The fact that Skipper was drunk was no excuse. Jill wore a smile on her face, which saddened him even more.

'I think we better go,' said Albert.

'Why don't you go?' said Skipper. 'If I go home sober to the wife, she'll have me at it all night and I won't be able to work on Monday.'

Jill laughed. 'Let's stay Albert, and don't be such a stick in the mud? You're only a young lad and you've plenty of years ahead of you for weeping and moaning.'

Skipper beamed. 'You remind me of my own mot, Albert. Every time I go home with a few pints on me, she's giving out. I tell her, you're giving out to me when I'm in a pub. When we're making love you have your eyes closed. You don't want to see me enjoying myself at all. Then she asks me, do I love her? And I tell her to act her age!'

Jill burst into a fit of laughter. The tears streamed down her cheeks.

'You're a gas man, Skipper. Get a drink Albert and have a bit of fun.'

'Albert wouldn't buy a drink. He comes from Limerick. You know, they're so mean down there that the seagulls carry a lunch pack when passing over it. I'm only joking you. Albert is one of the best.'

Albert stood up, but was not sure his legs would carry him. He was hot and cold, boiling and freezing, and both feelings hurt equally. He made his way to the bar and looked back down towards them. Skipper had his right hand on her shoulder and they were in hysterics of laughter. Jill looked up and caught the frightened look on Albert's face. She stopped laughing and stared vacantly at him. Without taking her eyes away, she removed Skipper's hand from her shoulder. It seemed the rest of the customers in the pub were aware something was wrong for the lounge fell silent.

Albert took his eyes away from Jill. He became conscious of someone else watching him. Yes. There was someone there at the far corner of the bar. He was a big, dark, devious looking man, with brown lurking eyes and a pinstripe suit. He looked almost like what Albert pictured the devil to be. He felt a coldness in his spine and turned and left quickly, moving as swiftly as was possible, fearing he might be followed by that loathsome-looking character.

*

The gods were against him too, for he was met in the street by a whirling wind and a driving rain thundering from the heavens. Now he understood the terrible power of fate which could quicken people's blood to suicide. He moved briskly through the driving rain, and when he reached home he locked the door firmly behind him. He sat silently on the bed. No tears would come, for he was more sick inside than any tear would have shown. The sounds from the derelict house harmonised with the winds, the airy sounds amplified through creaking doors and windows. The whole building seemed to be giving way to the pelting rain, almost about to burst in at any moment.

Through the raging and creaking sounds he could hear footsteps coming up the stairs. Then there was a knock on the

23

door. His heart stopped, momentarily. He held his breath and looked up. Should he play silent, until another knock came? He stood up, walked slowly towards the door and opened it.

An elderly gentleman stood in the darkness of the landing. He removed his cap, revealing his bald head.

'Sorry for disturbing you, my young man. The name's Peter Mulligan. I was told you just moved in. I'm your neighbour just below you. Terrible night. It was my good wife saw you, asked me to call up. Sometimes it can be quite lonely at first when moving in. From the country are you?'

'Limerick, yes. Albert Cagney is the name. Would you like to come in?'

'Ah, sure maybe for a minute. You don't happen to know what won the 4.30 at Newbury by any chance?'

'I'm sorry, I don't follow them. A cup of tea?'

'I should think not, it runs through my bowels. I much prefer stronger beverages. But alas; I am at present on what they call the wagon.'

'Is it just yourself and your wife live down stairs, or have you children?'

'No. Just the two of us. Fifteen years now and quite happily married. Mind you I'm not so sure she is. Give them plenty to eat. Would you like something solid, I always ask her. And sure once you give them plenty of that, there's little to complain about. I should think so. I must admit, I'm more than fond of a few drinks. I promised her I'd give it a miss for a year, and I'm a man of my word.'

'I must admit I take a drink myself.'

Peter's eyes lit up with enthusiasm. 'Do you fancy going down now for a couple of pints?'

'No, thank you.'

A look of disappointment creased Peter's face as he was deprived of an excuse for going on the tear.

He drifted aimlessly around the room, eventually stopping at some books.

'I see you like to read. Plays and poetry. You like that sort of stuff. The Quare Fellow. Our own sweet Brendan Behan. Drank with him for years in McDaid's Public House. In fact it was himself painted the John downstairs for a couple of pints.'

Albert listened with awe on the mention of the playwright. He suddenly forgot about his hurt. 'I'd love to meet Brendan Behan.'

'It's possible you will meet him too – pending which way you go in the next life. Unfortunately, he passed away a small few years ago. We had treasured times together. I had a car accident. I'm afraid Brendan wasn't around to reap the rewards, though plenty were. The only bank interested in my fortunes was the new Bank of America in Leeson Street. The manager put out the red carpet for me when I got the big cheque. I'll tell you he wasn't long about whipping the carpet up when a cheque hopped in O'Donoghues Public House as short as three months later.'

Peter went on talking until Albert could scarcely keep his eyes open. He did not know what to make of his neighbour, yet was momentarily pleased with the distraction from the earlier happenings.

'I see you're tired. I should think we're both tired. With me, it's the advancing years. I'm a terrible man, when I start talking. It keeps my mind at ease when I'm away from the beverage. Sometimes it gives me the urge. Be God, I think I'll go down now and try one. Are you sure you won't join me?'

Looking at his watch, he went skipping out of the room and down the stairs with the same urgency as a child does on a Christmas morning. Albert lay on his bed, and tried to read, although the early part of the evening haunted his brain. He eventually fell asleep.

*

Albert woke with a startled jerk at the sound of his doorbell ringing. It was five in the morning. He pulled his night-gown over him, and fearfully headed down the stairs. When he opened the front door, Jill was standing there.

'Can I come in? I need to speak to you.'

She looked different: untidy, worn, lost. A host of thoughts entered Albert's head. His eyes had been half-closed and sleepy; but now he felt wide-awake as he watched her stagger her way up the stairs.

'I suppose you want a cup of tea,' he said.

'Look, about Skipper—'

'I don't want to know.'

Jill stepped in sternly. 'Is that supposed to mean we're finished?'

Albert made no reply. His mind was numbed to any form of sympathy. There was a silence. He felt cheated; yet he thought he held the trump card when he said nothing.

Jill spoke. 'You're doing your best to make me feel as uncomfortable as possible?'

'No. But then you didn't make me feel too comfortable last night.'

'Look, I don't even know you and you're acting as if I was fucking married to you!' She continued to talk, with increasing speed and projection. 'I'm only out for a good time! You're so serious – don't you like a laugh? I had a drink on me, I'll have you know! I'm a big girl. I'm Jill, and I fell down the hill a long time ago!' She suddenly softened from her outburst, and fell almost into tears. 'I was going to change, for you. You know nothing, but I thought you were going to teach me something. I thought I could change, that you had given me a reason to. Do you want to go to bed with me?'

'No.'

Jill opened her handbag, and took out five pounds. She threw the money on the chair. 'Then piss off. I'll let myself out. Good riddance.'

She was gone.

Albert did not follow her. He sat in a chair and listened to her footsteps as she went down the stairs. The dawn light swept through the room like a spotlight. He was glad she had come back and apologized, but he was jealous of Skipper. When God closes one door, he opens another; that was the way it would be for Jill. He could not sleep now. He made a cup of tea.

6.

'Things is very quiet for a Monday morning,' Peader said. 'Be God, that's a right black eye you've got there, Skipper. Were you in a fight? Ha ha the wife did that, didn't she?'

Albert never looked up.

'Are yous all suffering from a hangover, or what?' said Peader.

'I got my bit of leg over,' Skipper said. 'I think Albert is suffering from the same'.

'Don't be bringing Albert into your dirty mind.'

'I met his bit of skirt on Saturday. He got a headache and went home. I know it's women usually get the headache, but when she met my irresistible charms she was cured. Her resistance eased. Furthermore she marked me ten out of ten and concluded by giving me a standing ovation. I'd say her hand was sore from all the clapping.'

'What's he on about?' said Peader. 'I think he's on drugs or fucking something.'

'Out sowing his oats,' Tim said.

'Sure he knows fuck all about farming,' said Peader. 'He only worries about his stomach – or what's hanging from it.'

There was a delighted cheer for the old man.

Albert tried to conceal his emotions, but in truth he was foaming at the mouth. He had never known Skipper to be so cruel and hurtful.

He stood up, walked towards the door and turned to Skipper. 'If you must know, I was talking to her yesterday and she said you were very small.' He stormed out of the office and out on to the Bond Road.

He was followed by simultaneous cries from inside.

'Good on you!'

'Fair play to you!'

'Good lad, Albert!'

Skipper ran out of the office leaving the door ajar, and shouted after Albert: 'If she had it hanging over her eye for a wart, I wonder would she call it small!'

*

Bond Road was just off the East Wall Road. It was reclaimed land from the sea. He walked towards the sea front. Papers, tins, bottles and garbage paved the shore. There was a pungent smell of carrion. The seagulls circled overhead like scavengers in search of a meal. The gentle but persuasive wind that sailed from the sea amplified the unpleasant odour; yet it also carried with it the fresh smell of the ocean. Albert passed through the seagulls out onto the barren shore. He saw an old gull that was scarcely able to walk let alone fly. There was no food near him and none of the other birds tried to help him. They just help themselves, he realised. Was life, in its many twists and turns, as cruel as that?

For him, it seemed that way as he headed back towards the McEwan's gate. The day would pass with lorry and tractor loads of timber from Foley's Carriers sweeping to and from the dockyards, where cargos landed daily from ships all over the world.

In the finish of work, he walked with Peader up the East Wall Road.

'I'll buy you a pint in the Wharf Tavern before we go home,' said Peader.

*

Albert listened as Peadar told about the dockers that would not work and about the halcyon days when he brought timber from Golden Lane to Manor Kilbride twice a day by horse and cart.

'Now, you see this pub. Of a Friday, you could buy anything from a needle to an elephant. All robbed from the ships of course. Anyway, everybody bought things. Except, of course, the bold Matt Talbot.'

'Did you know him?'

'Of course I knew him! Didn't I work with him in T and C Martin's for years? This woman was writing a book about him, and she came calling to me asking what I knew of him. Sure the man was obviously a very holy man, but then who isn't? I goes to mass every Sunday. I goes to visit me retarded daughter every Sunday and stays there for three hours looking at one another having nothing to say. And God help the poor girl, for she's a grand one. You see these fuckers driving in in their big cars, giving the nurses ten cigarettes to give to their kids and tells them they'll see them the next time they're in. I come in the next day to work. Now Matt Talbot, for instance, would be kneeling in the plywood shed praying when he should have been working. Do you understand? I was doing his donkey work. I mean he should have been working and doing his praying afterwards. Now as regards putting chains around himself – I suppose to try and kill himself – sure that's suicide. I know if I told anyone I was going to bind myself up in chains, they call me a fucking madman. Now, the mot has great faith in Matt Talbot. She's goes to mass every morning and lights a candle for her intentions. Probably to get rid of me. Ha ha ha, but sure she knows fuck all.'

7

After two days on the Bond Road the cargo was finished and it was back to the main office. Albert looked at Eamonn, who gave him a smile. He wondered: should he confide his secret about Jill to him and get his advice?

If he did not tell Eamonn, there was only Anthony, who smoked cigarettes with the dependence of a man sucking oxygen from a life-support machine. He was not quick with humour, but was quick to laugh with those that were. He shared weekends with Albert and Davey in the mountains. Cigarette smoking was prohibited in the office, so smokers had to go to a small toilet shed. Anthony spent considerable time there to feed his ongoing habit. As a result, staff referred to it as Anthony's Hole. On one occasion in the self-same place, someone had deposited what could only be described as a large French stick into the toilet with no success of flushing it down. It had become a source of gossip among the staff. There was speculation as to the identity of the culprit since nobody owned up. The first concern for the person who dropped such a missile was to their health. All eyes were on anyone unwell or with a different walk than usual, perhaps causing pain. The culprit was never found, but because of his He-Man structure it was generally assumed to be Eamonn. He had acquired the nickname, 'The Phantom Crapper'.

Mr Broderick stood with his back to the radiator giving the occasional cough to let his flock know that the Shepherd had them in his sights. He was a medium block of a man, with thin black

31

hair that was bald at the summit. It was seldom that anyone got the better of him. In the mid-sixties, authority played a major part in keeping employees under control. As a result, Mr Broderick liked to appear in the office without warning to give people a sudden jolt. By habit, his right hand was constantly in motion: first to his forehead, then across his head, and finally into his right pocket. When his hand arrived here, he would swivel on the balls of his feet. For this reason, he was generally known amongst the employees as 'Scratchy'.

Albert thought about him nervously. He was in awe of how Eamonn had bravely led the request for wage increases earlier in the year.

He remember Eamonn soldiering his way up to the office door. The gentle knock.

'Come in!' Mr. Broderick's command was boisterous but with a tone of being slightly taken aback at the intrusion.

Outside, all the other workers had listened in silence as they awaited their turn to enter the dreaded chamber. They prepared their speeches as flawlessly as was possible for delivery to such a dictator.

Eamonn opened the account. 'Happy New Year to you.'

'Is it that time of year, already?'

'It is. I suppose you know the reason for my visit.'

'No, actually.'

'Well, Mr Broderick. January the first. The time for increases in wages.'

'Ho ho ho.' He smirked like Santa Claus. 'I had quite forgotten.'

Conveniently forgotten you little fat bollocks, Eamonn thought to himself.

'Yes. Must get around to discussing it at board level,' Broderick said. 'But, no doubt it will be forthcoming. In the near future.'

After Eamonn's exit with a disgruntled smile, the procession started one after the other from Anthony right down to Albert. Each new contestant had been greeted with amazement from Mr Broderick. 'Is it that time of year already?'

Now, months later, no increase had come. Eamonn had made a number of reminders.

Suddenly Mr Broderick walked into his office and called out in a military voice. 'Eamonn!'

Eamonn entered.

When the door was closed firmly behind him, Mr Broderick began. 'After careful consideration, and because you are a senior, the company sees fit to increase you ten. We've not had a good year. But look at your progress as an arduous uphill grind, slow but getting there.' He spoke with a wry smile.

'On the contrary. I was reading the company did very well last year.'

He gave an awkward cough, followed by a nervous laugh. 'Must have been a misprint. What paper do you read?'

'The Observer.'

'You must bring me in that. By the way,' he whispered as though giving the secret winning number to the Irish Sweepstakes, 'it's back dated six weeks.'

'I'm very pleased, Mr Broderick, and I shall look forward to that extra seventy pounds next week.'

'Ten shillings a week is the increase.' He scratched his balls with more ferocity than usual.

'I thought you meant ten pounds a week. That's somewhat different. I shall have to buy The Observer more often, there seems to be plenty of vacancies. We must be on the look out.'

'Oh, we should always be on the look out, Eamonn.'

'I wasn't thinking about myself. I was thinking about you.'

'What?'

'What I mean is, if the increases are so low I'm sure with your leadership you could command a fine post anywhere.'

When Eamonn returned to work, he whispered to Albert. 'He wouldn't get a job on a poultry farm, chewing the slop for gummy chickens, the ignorant pig—'

'Perhaps,' Mr Broderick called out from his office, stopping him in his stride, 'I'll take it on myself to give you a pound!'

And so the sequence of the increases went every year.

Albert looked up at Eamonn.

'We'll go to the Neptune Rowing Club, Friday, Albert.'

*

The Neptune Rowing club was on the banks of the river Liffey. It was originally a boathouse, but had been converted into a cosy little Folk Club pub. There was a revolution of folk protest songs in the sixties, and here the best Irish acts could be seen. Johnny Moynihan, Al O'Donnell, Dave Smith and Gay Corcoran, Luke Kelly, Frank Harte, Andy Irvine and Terry Woods and more.

'Were you ever in love, Eamonn?'

'Only with myself, Albert.'

'What would you do if you were with a girl, like, and she was going with you, but you knew others were at her?'

'You mean a gangbang?'

'No.'

'I'd break their fucking necks and probably hers as well.'

Albert would have to leave his questioning for another time.

*

After bidding Eamonn goodnight on the quays, he headed home. As he approached Leeson Street, he was taken aback by the presence of a girl standing outside his flat. He walked briskly towards her, squinting in an effort to focus more clearly. Yes, it was Jill. She stood by the steps leading to the front door as he approached her. She stared, lost, vacantly, into his eyes and then ran and threw her arms around his neck and kissed him. Intermingled in her eyes were tears of joy and sorrow, the mixed feelings of being lost and found. They made their way up to the room and never spoke a word, but there were words in the silences. They left the light off; the stars multiplied into myriads through the window and the moon sent a blue film of light through his room. He turned towards her, and she came close to him, and they kissed. Slowly, in one another's arms, they burst into extreme ecstasy together like a volcano.

Afterwards they lay together, feeling like milk on a low fire boiling over in paradise. She fell asleep, and he watched her face in the moonlight. Surely all their problems were at rest, and peace and tranquillity were there for the night that was in it. He drifted off at last.

When he awoke, he was alone. Jill had left without waking him.

8

The sound of their boots in the multicoloured, faded leaves. Crickets singing among the grass and the waving poppies. They proceeded on the long, circuitous country road from Donard to the Glen of Imaal. The insects were unaware of the two human forms of Albert and Davey. Around them were those dark mountains, from Table to Lugnaquilla with orange, red and yellow colours spilling from the sun and electrifying the sky. It was what must be to every poet and painter a paradise.

Albert had come to these parts of the country since he was thirteen, and each time was more mesmerised by the magic of these mountains and the many different sunsets.

They took a short cut through an aged but beautiful forest, across the yellow meadows, until they met the Slaney River. Talking, laughing, and throwing stones into the virgin waters. Splashing each other as they negotiated the stepping stones, which distracted the free flowing river, the water tossing and making white waves and turning into currents as it freed itself. Then they continued out past a farmer's yard and on to a botharín that led to the Seskin Pub.

Here was the Fenton's cottage with the pub attached, with its green corrugated roof. They could see it as they approached from a far distance. Inside, with its sheeted timber ceiling and concrete floor, the pub looked like an army barracks. It was not the country landscape alone that excited the youths, but the country folk also. They met great characters on their visits, ordinary people in their own environments, foresters, farmers, people who worked on the local woodworking mill. The Department of Defence owned most of the land that stretched from Cameragh hill at the foot of Lug Mountain to the great Sugarloaf. It was used as a training ground for the army who were stationed for training periods at Coolmooney Camp, just a mile from Fenton's pub. So apart from the campers, hikers, climbers, hostellers, a lot of soldiers spent their recreation time in the pub.

'Ah! Albert, Davey.' They were greeted by Maurice, a local lad they knew over their many visits.

'Maurice, Ned, Pat, how are you?' said Albert, looking around. 'Let's sit down here.'

They sat in front of the bar after getting their drinks. Apart from the occasional locals at the bar, there were some soldiers playing cards on a table just before the dartboard. Albert noticed Skipper playing darts with some of his climbing friends.

'Hello Albert and Davey!' said Bernie Fenton, the owner. 'How are you? I didn't notice you coming in. God! Wasn't that terrible about that poor cyclist?'

'We didn't hear.'

'Apparently she fell from her bike coming down the hill in Ballinclea and hit her head on a rock. The poor child was dead before they got her to the hospital. Terrible isn't it? Hey Maurice, we'll get a game of darts going with the lads here.'

'We'll play later.'

Skipper walked towards Albert. 'Did you hear about Donal? I called in to his house to see was he coming away and he was stripping the wallpaper. Are you changing the wallpaper, I asked him. No, says he. I'm moving house.'

'Ah fuck off,' said Donal. 'Don't mind him Albert. It's his round anyway. Come on, you bollix, it's your throw.'

The door opened, and in walked the strangest looking

gentleman Albert and Davey had seen. He was in his mid sixties, with beady eyes and a brownish whiskey nose. He wore a fisherman's hat and spoke as though everyone in the pub was deaf, delivering each word with slow pronounced accuracy.

'Inclement sort of weather,' he said to Mrs Fenton.

Everyone in the bar came to a standstill in an effort to observe the odd looking gentleman.

'What will it be, sir?' said Mrs Fenton.

'Something strong I imagine, to refurbish my system to a more natural state after an exhausting journey over the hills. A large Jameson would, I think, be the answer.'

'You're a stranger around these parts!'

'Perrim's the name Ma'am. Professor Leonard McDonald Perrim. I'm here to report for a newspaper the unfortunate circumstances surrounding the young woman's death. You are, I dare say, familiar with what happened.'

'She fell from her bike coming down a hill in Ballinclea.'

The Professor paid for his drink and sat down beside Albert and Davey. 'I'll sit here, if you don't mind. I'm nearly exhausted after a long journey. God be with the halcyon days when I was young and eager to pit my strength against the hills. You two young lads are well able for such challenges, no doubt? Do you mind if I ask your names?'

'This is Albert and my name is Davey. Were you walking?'

'Push bike. You'll have a drink, I dare say?'

Davey was making efforts at holding in laughter. Skipper had a bemused look on his face, occasionally glancing down at Albert as he paced up and down playing darts.

'Jaysis, Albert. He's on a pushbike. I can hardly walk up those hills.'

'Here you are, my good friends.'

'Are you from these parts, sir?'

'I come from Clifton. I've spent a number of holidays in

Rathdangan with a cousin of mine, who has since passed away. I decided to purchase a cottage just outside Rathdangan to spend the rest of my days in peace. I'm seventy now, and not unhappy. I'm near the end of the road. You two young lads are only on the road to combating all the trials you'll have to encounter on your passage through this life. But, no doubt, you're well able for it.'

'Are you married?'

'No. I never did take the plunge. But still on the lookout.'

Davey burst into laughter, as did the Professor. Albert was nudging Davey to control himself.

Skipper arrived with three drinks. 'Here's a gargle, Professor, and two pints for my mates.'

'You must allow me to pay for them.'

'They're already paid for.'

'Then give all in the house a drink!' shouted the Professor.

All momentarily came to a standstill.

'I would, if I may,' said the Professor, 'like a quiet place where I can compose this article which my newspaper is waiting for.'

'You can use the kitchen,' said Mrs Fenton. 'George, show the Professor where the kitchen is.'

When the Professor left, Albert turned furiously to Davey. 'What are you laughing at that auld lad for? That fella's a queer! And do you see the way he keeps looking at you?'

'So what, I'm only enjoying myself.'

Skipper called Albert to one side. Albert hesitated to get up for him, but the drink had diluted his anger.

'Look,' said Skipper, 'I'm sorry about last Saturday. I know I was drunk, but I knew what I was doing. You asked me to help you, and that I did. She's not for you. You've got more pedigree than mixing with the likes of her. You can get more women than de Valera can get votes. Do you think I'm fucking mad? I didn't want to go home with my dick on a sling. That one has seen enough of them to make a rope between here and the top of lug ten times over. I never went near her. I've more respect for my Percy. I'll talk to you again. Come on, play a game of darts. Are you playing, Davey?'

'I'll just sit here, and polish off these few pints.'

'Hey Davey,' said Albert, 'you mind that auld queer when he comes out, and don't go talking to him.'

'I'm only taking the piss out of him.'

'That's what Albert is afraid of,' said Skipper.

'Quit that messing, Skipper,' said Mrs Fenton. 'Are you playing Maurice?'

'I'm in.'

'Maurice and Skipper can only have two lives; they're too good. Sixpence a head.'

Albert was not good at darts, but Skipper had carefully pinned off everybody else leaving himself and Albert in the final. Then he purposely missed Albert's number to let him win. Albert felt Skipper was sorry now for what he had done with Jill in the Pembroke. He could see how popular Skipper was amongst the crowd. Albert's thoughts turned to Jill. The thought of her didn't seem to hurt that much now while he was out here in the country; here he felt less entangled in the magnetic phenomenon of his attraction to her.

The Professor emerged from the kitchen door. 'The telephone. I would appreciate quietness for the duration of this call.'

The telephone was at the end of the bar, and with the aid of Mrs Fenton, he got through to the editor's office. He spoke in a thunderous voice. Everyone save himself fell silent.

'…while negotiating a steep decline… it appears with such ferocity, she lost her equilibrium and was dislodged from the pedals… depositing herself in the mire….'

Skipper had just taken a mouthful of drink when he suffered a sudden outburst of laughter. His inward suction battled with his outward, causing nearby companions to suffer a spray of second-hand Guinness.

'Did you ever hear such longwinded bullshit in your life?' he said to Albert.

Albert smiled. He could not have imagined he could have given way to Skipper after what had happened. Skipper still wore the marks of two black eyes but Albert was still not prepared to ask what happened, though the drink had suppressed the evil hatred he had felt only a few days before. Albert looked over at Davey, who was talking to the Professor. Davey was laughing, and every now and again the Professor would grasp his hand. Albert looked on in shocked bewilderment.

'Hey Professor,' Skipper said, 'are you playing a game of darts? I'd say you could throw a fair dart.'

'I've played a game in my time. What are the stakes? Shall we say ten bob?'

Davey was laughing. For the sake of Albert, he pointed with his eyes at his hand, which was held by the Professor.

Albert turned a cherry colour and walked over to the Professor. 'Take your dirty hands, off him. We can do without your type in here.'

'He's right, old man. These lads are only children,' Skipper said.

'I'm getting out of here,' said Albert. 'Are you coming, Davey?'

*

The two youths left the pub. The full moon made the night seem like twilight. They walked the country roads and through the forest towards Stranahealy shack in silence. The moonbeam gave blue films of light as it shot through the palm trees. The night flies danced and glittered, alert at the sound of their steps on the damp peat. Their breath turned to mist in the cold air. There was the

41

occasional hooting of an owl, or the sound of a wild deer dashing away in the darkness.

Stranahealy shack, as it was known, was three miles from Fenton's pub. It was a big two-story house with eight rooms, apparently owned in the past by someone of that name. Although derelict, it still boasted a good roof, doors, shutters on the windows, and wooden floors in some of the rooms. The foresters used it as a canteen when taking a break from work during their day. One room had an iron bed in it, brought there by mountaineers in the past. Albert lit a fire in the fireplace to cook some food, while Davey was busily occupied catching a bat. He had stripped himself to the waist and made a net from his string vest.

'Got you! Look Albert, he's like a bleeding mouse when he takes his wings in. I see you and Skipper made up your differences. Do you know what the Professor told me? That we could stay in his house in Rathdangan anytime we like.'

'I told you Davey, I think he's a queer. Do you know what they get up to?'

'Yeah. Well maybe.'

'We'll walk over Table Mountain tomorrow. Come on, we'll hit the sack.'

They slept on the iron bed in their sleeping bags, using their rucksacks as pillows. In the early morning, they were awakened by the chirping of the birds nestling beside a hole in the roof.

The sun shone down on the way up Table Mountain, but a cool breeze fanned their temperatures making the hard walking pleasant. They sat to rest on the incline before attacking the summit.

'This is beautiful,' Davey said.

They could see over the Spinks and the giant landscape of the valley, with a silver river running from the hills. A mist rose from the top of the mountains giving a purple effect, and there was a smell of common gorse. To Albert and Davey, these were heavenly sights and smells. Albert watched his companion as they surveyed the surroundings. He had wished he had inherited those good looks Davey had. He was a little jealous of him. He wondered which of God's creations was the most perfect, humanity or nature. They competed in their majesty and it was a harmonious struggle, as both co-operated in complimenting God's genius.

'Don't ever mix or call around to anyone like the Professor Davey!'

'Ha! Listen, nobody will make a fool of me!'

They continued on their walk into the mild autumn evening.

9

'What a love nest!' said Skipper as he paced around the flat. 'I never saw the like of it. Sure this is a devil's paradise! I'd pay half the rent with you if I only got to use it one hour a night. I hope you don't get into trouble paying for it; both of us could be out of work any day.'

'I'll sort that out,' said Albert. 'You said you'd explain for me? You can use this place anytime if you'll tell the doctor for me.'

'You're drawing water okay? Did you take a furtive look? No sign of scabs or the like? I'd say you're all right. Mind you, if you get a whack of a dose you'll have to go around with your own soap and towel for six months. You'll have to turn this place into a monastery and nurse yourself with salve until you get the okay. Come on, we'll get going.'

*

Albert said nothing as they made their way to the Adelaide hospital. His mind was in a state of confusion. He trembled as they walked, thinking of the consequences should he have caught an infection from Jill.

When they reached the hospital, Skipper spoke to the nurse who was standing next to a porter.

'Pardon me miss, where can we see a doctor?'

'Doctor Maher, is it?'

'I don't know.'

'Have you an appointment? What's the problem?'

'It's kind of personal,' said Albert.

She smiled. 'We are well versed in personal matters in the hospital. So, come on. Out with it.'

'Will I ask the porter to leave?' Skipper whispered to Albert. 'She wants you to exhibit your goods here in the hallway. I hope Percy is in repose. She's not a bad looking nurse.'

The blood rushed to Albert's face. He turned and walked a few steps away.

'Nurse, you understand, it's my friend here,' said Skipper loudly. 'You see he had a few drinks on him the other night, and he met with this girl who apparently had less morals than a donkey would have in a field of asses. He's a bit embarrassed. It's only when the drink is on him, you understand, that the stallion comes out.'

'Follow me.' The nurse smiled and led them to the waiting room. There were three other men in the room.

Albert and Skipper sat opposite.

Skipper whispered. 'See your man over there, coughing? Pretending to have pneumonia? He has a doze of the clappers, the same as the rest of them. Sure look at the rash – it's coming out above his collar, right on his neck.'

'Shut up Skipper.'

10

Albert breathed a sigh of relief when the doctor told him it was unlikely he had an infection. They left the hospital and walked to O'Dwyer's Public House.

'What happened that you're displaying those black eyes?'

'Yeah, that's what I'm trying to figure out. All I remember's that it was that famous night in the Pembroke. This big dark eyed fucker with two of his mates followed me. I was too drunk to know what I said. All I know is I ended up on the ground after I had got a fair clobbering. I told Jill I fell. Next I was in a taxi on my own having just woken up from a sleep. I'll find out who that bollix is and sort him out. I'll have to have a talk with Jill, see can she remember.'

'Are you going to continue on in the Acting Academy?'

'That's only a money-making racket. I'm going to direct a play myself. The Plough and the Stars. I'm going to get you to play the Young Covey.'

Peter Mulligan, Albert's neighbour from downstairs, came in and walked towards them.

'My excellent young men, and how are we all today? All muscles moving, I expect.'

'Hello Mr Mulligan. This is Skipper McCabe. I mean, Christy.'

'I should think it best if we seal this encounter with a drink.'

'This man drank with Brendan Behan.'

The local guard burst in on the scene. He was followed by a rough looking man. Both were drunk, and there was a peculiar aroma of stale fish, eggs and foul underpants.

The guard was a chubby man of medium height with a big beer belly. He spoke with a gravelly Dublin voice. 'Come here, how's it going Mulligan? How's your tank? Don't fucking tell me you're not carrying. Slip us a fucking score there. This is Terry. He's a binman, but he's no fucking brains.'

'Fuck off Larry. You wait and see. I'll be driving a Rover in a couple of years.'

'Yeah, a robbed one.'

'No. I'll be running one.'

'Running after one, thumbing a lift.'

'No. I'll be racing.'

'Yeah, pigeons from Dolphin's Barn flats. Larry Coyne is the name. If you're in a spot of bother, give us a shout. As long as it's not murder or rape. What this your names are? Where do yous work? Where abouts are you from? Where are yous living? Here, give us two pints. Binman, you're paying for them.

'Keep your voice down,' ordered the barman.

'Here. You just pull the pints and mind your own business if you want your shop open next week. Have you a light on your pushbike? What time do you close at? Don't be too smart. We've our own fucking ways. Just pour the two pints.'

'I'm Albert, and this is Christy.'

'Here, Binman? You sit down there and write a thesis on Einstein's Theory of Relativity, and pay for those two pints.'

'Don't forget, Larry, you're only a guard.'

'Shut up, for fucks sake. Hey, Mulligan? I have a tip for a horse. Keep it to yourself.'

Terry sat beside Albert. Skipper, Peter, and Larry conversed about horses.

'Albert, isn't that your name?'

'Yes.'

'My name is Terry Kiely. Don't mind that guard. I'm not an

47

intelligent bloke, but I know enough to never trust a guard or a barman. They'd fucking rob you. Always remember that! Do you know the answer to the question? I'd love to give it to him to sicken him. Do you know what I mean?'

'I don't know the answer to the question, Terry.'

'Do you know when you've a hundred pairs of socks, and your mother washes them? You know when you go looking for a pair, you can never find a pair that match? One of the pair is always missing. I wonder would that have anything to do with it?'

'I wouldn't say so.'

'Or, do you know all the space the birds have in the sky. How is it that when they shit, it's always on somebody's head? Could that be it?'

'I would say definitely not.'

'Do you see your man over there coming in with the dog? We'll that's the toucher Nelson. He's worse than a guard, and that's saying a lot. He'll be over here in a minute. Although, you've got to hand it to him, in his own way he's a smart fucker. Do you know what I saw him doing one day? There's a shop around the corner, Grogan's it's called. Well the toucher carries a tin opener with him wherever he goes. When he gets a good few bob from touching, he goes into Grogan's shop and orders six slices of ham and a tin of dog food for his dog. One day I was in the shop, and he had his messages. Well this old toff was in the shop at the time. What does the toucher do, but start to open the dog food in front of her. You're not going to eat that, says she in a posh voice. Not all of it ma'am, says he. I'm going to give some to the dog. A smart fucker. She ended up giving him five pounds.' Terry took a swig of his pint. 'Are you going with a mot?'

Albert thought for an instant about Jill. 'Sort of.'

'Nice to be nice. But take my advice. Get them young, treat them rough, and tell them fuck all. Sure they'll find out anyway. Do you know what I mean?'

48

'Here Einstein. Are you backing this horse?'

'Listen guard, I don't back horses. That's the reason I always have money for drink. Ah fuck it, here, I'll put five pounds on it. What's it called?'

'Jill's First. Keep it to yourself.'

Albert's heart received a jolt. He looked up at Skipper to see if this name had being sold to them for a prank.

'Isn't that a coincidence?' Skipper said. He had come down to reassure Albert. 'Swear, I never mentioned her. Do you want to stick a few bob on her?'

'Yes, here's a pound, but I'm going home.'

'Are you having another gargle before you go?'

'I'll get it,' said Terry, brandishing a wad of notes that would choke an elephant.

'Have we gathered the foliage for the encounter?' Peter said. 'Lest the animal may hear of our uncertainty and decide to put a halt to his gallop until a later date. I mean it's five to fucking three.' He got up to go to the toilet.

'Okay,' said Larry. 'That's thirty three pounds. I'm going over.'

'Albert,' Skipper said, 'I put a fiver on between the two of us. I was carrying a few quid.'

There was a tense silence as all waited for Larry to return. All eyes were focused on the doorway entrance. Remembering the doctor's verdict, Albert breathed sigh of relief and his heart lifted again. A thrill entered his body as he toyed with the idea of calling up to her. Skipper did say he never went near her. But then, did he believe him?

Skipper had tried to make amends on a number of occasions. Albert recalled that he had made a conscious decision to forget her.

The entrance door burst open, and the boisterous, turbulent, flat Dublin accent of Larry screamed out. 'Take it out of that! You're dealing with no gobshite here! What did I fucking tell you? Romped home at 16-1! Yous are buying for the rest of the night! Leave it to Larry!'

Peter Mulligan and Skipper ran to the exit to seek confirmation of the guard's claim, knowing that home truths were not amongst his strong points – if he had any.

The toucher Nelson had a field day, and on top of the good fortune of getting legless without paying a cent, he went out into the street with more than six pounds. The proprietor of the establishment had just entered and was hit by a wall of drunken bombardment, along with a rare rendering of 'Pidgeon on the Gate' from Peter on the tin whistle. He ordered the entertainer and his troupe to leave immediately and not return.

Larry lumbered towards the owner, spiting and farting on his way, and incoherently tried to explain that he was a guard. As he rumbled unintelligibly the owner gradually flared red and began shouting that his tolerance for bullshit was evaporating and he was calling the guards.

Not to appear defeated amongst his fellow folk, Larry turned as they exited and delivered lines he could say drunk or sober because he used them so often.

'Well then. Fuck you and your old kip, anyway. Because that's all it is.'

11.

A fiver was shoved into the taxi-man's hand. He was told to stop complaining about the singing and to give a hand to hoist a feast of steak and kidney pies and drink into the boot of the taxi. The goods had been purchased by Larry after he had made a collection from all concerned. From there it was decided to go back to Peter's flat. Little thought was given to what his good wife might think when she would encounter the strange gathering. Fortunately for her, she was out and Peter had forgotten his keys. Because it took such an effort to negotiate the stairs in their state, and a further journey was beyond endurance, Peter bellowed that they make one more flight upstairs to Albert's room.

Not too many words were spoken; steak and kidneys pies were swallowed with savage gusto and then it was back to more drink.

'You need the dry filling in the pit of the stomach,' Peter exclaimed as he poured himself a tumbler of whiskey.

Terry was asleep on a chair with half a half-eaten steak and kidney pie dribbling on his lap.

'Keep fucking quiet will yous!' roared Larry. 'Remember you're not in your own place now! Will someone sing a song?'

He was the loudest of all.

Skipper gave a fair rendering of 'The Rocks of Bawn'. When he finished his feed, Peter took out his whistle again and played a couple of reels. Albert alone heard the doorbell ring. He made his way to answer it unnoticed, and passed down the long stairway to the main hall door. To his surprise, Jill stood outside with a

51

stranger.

'We were passing and just rang, thought you might be in. By the way this girl has a flat, next to mine. Her name is Eve. Eve, this is Albert.'

Albert turned his eyes from Jill and focused on the other lady. Ebony hair with dark seductive eyes and baby bronze skin. She was a beauty beyond his comprehension. If ever there was one, she was an icon of female perfection. He shook her petite hand.

'There's a neighbour upstairs with friends and they're all drunk. Do you want to come up?'

'Yeah, if you don't mind. But if it's a personal party, we'll see you again.'

'Skipper's there.'

Albert led the way up to the room while the two girls followed. There was a stunned silence when the girls made an appearance in the room.

Then Larry spoke. 'Sorry misses, we didn't know Albert was expecting company. We had a touch on the horses and brought back a few drinks. We were just singing a few songs. What will you have?'

Jill went to get drinks, while Albert indicated to Eve the sofa was free, because Peter had got up and removed his hat and Terry had fallen from same, wedging the steak and kidney pie between himself and the floor. Eve sat down with Jill when she returned with the drinks.

Albert poured himself a glass of ale and was standing beside Skipper. 'Ah, Skipper. If you want Jill as a girlfriend, it's okay with me.'

Peter, being as charming and as sober as was possible, spoke to the girls. 'Would one of you good ladies oblige us with a song?'

'I will,' said Eve.

Albert's heart melted as Eve sang 'Sweet Carnlough Bay'. Her soft and lilting voice carried through the air more pleasantly than a linnet singing on a clear morning.

The gathering voiced the general consensus. 'More! More! More!'

So Eve followed with 'Mary from Dungloe'.

When she had finished, she looked at Albert and asked him to sing. Her alluring voice was a summons to his heart, so as best as he could he sang 'The Parting Glass'.

Just as the songs were finally bringing sanity and tranquillity to the assembly, Skipper asked Jill and Eve in as quiet and inaudible a voice as was possible if they would escape with Albert and himself to Corrigan's Pub.

'Good idea!' blasted Larry. 'We'll all go to the pub!' He gave skipper a look that made it evident that trying to bail out without his knowledge was like trying to sneak out two elephants from the zoo in the back of a small car.

So all retired to Corrigan's.

*

An hour and a half passed until Albert finally asked if Eve would like to take a walk and get some air.

'You get fed up with the pub scene, after a time,' Eve said. 'It's nice to get some air'.

'Yes. I do too.'

They were strolling aimlessly up the street.

'What age are you?'

'I'm twenty-one,' Albert lied.

'Me. I'm twenty-four. Do you want to come back to my flat?'

Albert's pulse began to race. He was about to ask her how much she charged, but decided he would wait. If she asked too much, he could lose sight of her. He wanted to savour her presence for as long as possible.

At her hall door, Albert finally plucked up the courage. 'How much do you charge, Eve?'

She smiled. Her whole face creased in a different dimension of magnetic splendour. Then she put her hand to her mouth and her smile continued into a childish giggle. Suddenly her composure returned. 'Do you usually get drunk, and then go out with prostitutes?'

'No,' he said.

This was more than embarrassing.

'Forty pounds.'

My God, he thought, that's five-weeks wages for a half an hour of ecstasy!

He recalled the teacher in school telling a story of a man selling his soul to the devil for ten years of worldly pleasure, after which time he was doomed for eternity. I'm doing the same thing thought Albert, for a half an hour. But then he came to reason – he was doomed already from his encounter with Jill.

'I'll give you five pounds, if I could have a cup of tea and just talk to you.'

'I was going to bring you in for tea anyway. You did bring me into your flat, and didn't charge.'

Her room was draped in the strangest pattern of colours. Albert suspected that this girl was a little different from the ordinary. He mused with excitement at the surroundings.

'I hope you're not mad at Jill or me,' said Eve, 'because she told me all about you.'

Albert felt the veins on his neck thicken. Had she been less than the Venus she was, he would have made an early exit through the nearest opening that could be found.

'What we really called for was to ask about the play you and your friend were doing. I'm very big into the arts. As you can see, I'm a painter. I wanted to see about getting a part. I'm sorry to disappoint you but I'm no prostitute, or I'm not on the game as Jill puts it.'

Why me, thought Albert? Why am I always caught wearing sunglasses when it's raining? Saying the wrong thing at the wrong time to the wrong person? He had shown his hand before he was ever asked.

'I don't go after prostitutes. That was just an accident, how I met Jill.'

Her eyes sparkled with a light that was the nearest thing to paradise Albert could have imagined.

'You don't have to explain to me. Everything's fine. Whatever you or Jill does is okay with me. I'm only into my paintings. And I pay no heed to anyone else's business. Would you like a joint?'

'A joint?'

'Ah! You don't smoke.'

'No.'

'Would you like to have a look at my paintings?'

'I'd love to.'

Eve walked him through a door of hanging beads into another room. 'Landscapes, and some portraits.'

'They are magnificent. My God, you're a genius.'

'Hardly, but thanks anyway. I'll make tea.'

The key in the main hall door could be heard turning.

'Are you home Eve?' Jill said from the hall.

'I am. Albert's here with me. Do you want to come in?'

'Skipper's with me.' Eve opened the door.

'Hello Eve and Albert!' Skipper said in a posh voice Albert never heard him use before. 'My God! That guard is something else! My constitution wouldn't be able to take much more of him. Jill tells me you're looking for a part in the play we're doing, Eve.'

'Yeah. That would be nice.'

Skipper sat down. 'Well we're going to hold a reading, as soon as we can establish where we're going to hold it.'

They drank tea and held idle conversation. Albert was anxious to leave, as he was aware of what Skipper was capable of saying in the company of females from past experience. The opportunity for such an event happening again was to be avoided.

'I'll see you again, sometime,' Eve said to Albert at the door.

Albert wanted to speak to her, but with the presence of the other two he felt he could not. He walked away with Skipper, and went back to his flat when Skipper got a taxi.

Twilight had set in, and fatigue was now his companion.

12.

Peader was holding court regarding the builders' strike.

'They're right to go on strike over wet time! It's alright for you, sitting in a shed, to say they shouldn't. But if you were on a building site and the rain running down into your underpants, you'd change your story!'

'Well,' Skipper said, 'if we have to go out with them we'll have more time to spend with women.'

'A fucking bear wouldn't hug you!' Peader said.

While he took a drink, the cup shook in his hand. A sudden jerk ran through his body, his eyes did a cartwheel and he fell sideways on the bench.

'Jaysis!' said Skipper. 'Are you alright Peader?'

There was no sounds coming as he tried to speak.

'Albert. Get an ambulance, quick!'

The ambulance arrived, and Peader was taken to the hospital.

*

Calls from the office phone were made and it was established that he was stable.

'Did you enjoy your day off, Albert?' Eamonn asked.

'Yes.'

Albert was not in form for talking, let alone working. Eve was his only day-dreaming companion. Her walk, her talk, the way she smiled were prisons to his labour. He would have to ensure that

57

Skipper would take Jill from his hands. It wasn't real love he had encountered with her; he could see that now. A phase, maybe. She had faded from his heart. A prostitute, he thought. How could he have done it? But warmness and a passion were taking place in his heart for Eve. The blood turned in his body as he recalled asking her how much she charged.

'Albert!'

Mr Broderick called from his office door. His voice swept through the office like thunder. A more realistic spirit jumped back into Albert's body and caused his pulse to motor with rapidity. A pin would have sounded like a cymbal if it fell to the floor. The silence frightened him. All eyes were focused on him and it seemed to him that they had all turned to stone, for it was not often that Mr Broderick called.

'Albert, I said!'

Albert got to his feet and turned towards the office. He could see the ghostly figure through the office window. He wore a sombre look; his right hand was held to his coughing mouth and his left hand was scratching his balls.

'Mr Broderick's calling you!' Eamonn said with a degree of urgency.

'Hey, Albert! Mr Broderick's wants you!' Anthony hissed.

'AHEM. Were you asleep, out there daydreaming or what? Do you hear me boy? Speak up, I say. You have to pull up your socks, now. Can you hear me?'

'Yes Mr Broderick sir.' And so can the entire office staff, Albert thought.

'I want to give you a different chance. See if you're capable. I'm going to give you a job making up the wages. Eamonn will show you what's to be done. Pay attention to him.'

'Yes, Mr Broderick. Thank you.'

He was shivering and Mr Broderick knew he had him on a rein. Could he find the courage to ask for a raise? If he did not, he would be the butt of all the office jokes. Eamonn faked a cough to let Albert know he was listening. Would he be a man or a mouse? He cast his mind up above for inspiration and courage: when it failed to come, he suddenly realized he wasn't on God's good books after his encounter with Jill.

'I'll be watching you with interest. That's it for now. Tell Eamonn, I want him.'

'Thank you.'

He turned to leave Mr Broderick's office. Anthony's face displayed a sardonic grin.

Albert turned back. 'Will I get an increase?'

Mr Broderick gave a wry smile, which seemed to rebel against the other features on his face, making him look cartoonish.

'After a trial, perhaps, I'll give it some consideration.'

Albert's heart put on the brakes and slowed down as he left his office.

*

A sigh of relief passed over the office when Eamonn told the staff that Scratchy had gone home. It was like a faith healing for the dumb. The stone statues once again began to talk and hum.

'Albert, I think we'll have to call you a wages clerk from now on,' Eamonn said. 'That's a big title. I could hear you weren't very successful in getting Scratchy to up the stakes. Him giving a raise at this time would be like him wanting to slide down a banisters and use his balls as brakes. Will we go and see how Peader is tonight? He's in Stephen's hospital. Anthony, will you come as well?'

'Okay.'

*

Albert was called to the trade counter just outside the main office. He was told there was a guard waiting to see him.

'That was a great night, last night! Peader told me where you worked. Jaysis! I know auld Peader from East Wall. Was it a stroke he had? His son's a docker. He races greyhounds, I was just talking to Skipper out in the yard and he was telling me. Listen, I'm looking for a bit of timber, cheap. I have to get a job done on the house, to get back in with the missus after last night. She looked at me this morning as though I had gangrene. I'd say Terry has a sore head this morning. I hope he doesn't leave half of my bin behind.'

Larry rambled on.

*

Peader was sitting with his head held up by a mountain of pillows as Albert, Anthony and Eamonn walked into the ward.

'Get me out of here, they're fucking starving me! And somebody is after snaring me pipe!'

There were six beds in the room, and all the others were occupied. They all seemed old to Albert, and it looked as though there was life-support apparatus beside most of them. There were stands with half-filled bottles hanging upside-down, with tubes heading in the direction of the unfortunate victims. A poignant smell of ether assured Albert this was not the nicest place to spend your last few days. The man lying next to Peader looked like the nearest thing to death he had ever seen. He lay there stretched out with eyes closed, and only the gentlest snore revealed that there was still life in him. But even the snore itself did not seem comfortable. It was rather like someone gasping for air, underwater.

'That man you're looking at is riddled with cancer,' Peader said loudly.

The sick man gave a few panicked snorts, and jumped up as if poked with a red-hot iron. The Lazarus-like resurrection caused Albert to move away with a jolt.

'I'll see you down, you auld bollix' he moaned through decrepit asthma. Then like Finnegan's dummy being thrown into the case, or a man shot by a firing squad, he fell back into repose.

Peader gave a broken, startled laugh, and then spoke in a whisper. 'That's the first time I saw him move since I came in.'

A nurse walked in with Skipper beside her.

'He's just there,' she said in a Cork accent as she pointed towards Peader.

'Do you mind me asking Nurse, are you married or in waiting?'

'I don't follow you.'

'Your name?'

'Nurse Levins,' she said shyly. 'Sandra.'

'Do you dance around, or what? Who's you favourite showband, The Royal or the Miami? Do you go to the Metrapole, or the National?'

'Johnny McEvoy.'

'Johnny McEvoy?'

'I love Johnny McEvoy signing 'Muirsheen Durkin'. God, I think he's great. Here's the doctor.'

A black doctor appeared on the scene beside Peader's bed, picking up his chart.

'And how you feel?'

'I'm starving, Doctor, and someone swiped me pipe.'

'We can't give you food. We operate tomorrow.'

'Would you ever heal his hole, Doctor?' said Skipper. 'I have to work with him, and when he gets rid of his lunch it's unbelievable.'

When the doctor left, Peader had turned white. Although his mouth was moving there were no words coming out.

Skipper was speaking from the end of the bed. 'I knew we shouldn't have let that Jack Lynch in. Importing cheap labour, from Africa.'

'I saw them on Pathé News,' said Anthony. 'They do their healing with a sharp slate, tied onto a piece of bamboo. And they yodel when they operate. They don't call it an operation, they call it a ceremony to their chief God Whackadoodee, or some fucking thing like that. What happens when he gets his hands on one of our sharp knives? I mean he can't even speak English!'

'I'm surprised at you, Anthony,' said Skipper. 'Laughing at that bollix. I always took you for a gentleman.'

Peader's voice had come back now, and he expressed his determination not to let anybody operate on him.

'I'm sorry, Skipper. I wasn't laughing at him. I was thinking of a joke I heard some time ago.'

'You're going to be fine, Peader,' Eamonn said. 'All you need is a bit of rest. You'll be up and about in a couple of days.'

'Where have you your money hid?' said Skipper. 'In case you do kick the bucket. We'll all go out and have a good night on you.'

The nurse had come in to tell them that visiting time was up.

'You knew who I was, all along.' said Skipper. 'That's how you said you liked Johnny McEvoy?'

'And who are you then?'

'You're embarrassing me now. Johnny McEvoy's brother!'

'O God! That's a fright. Tell him I was asking for him. But don't tell him I'm fat!'

'You're not fat nurse. Don't let anyone ever tell you your fat. You're what's called pleasantly plump.'

'Thank you.'

The fat nurse stood in the hallway with a slight tilt of her head and a favourable smile, and the boys bid her goodnight in passing her. Skipper was humming 'Muirsheen Durkin' as they continued along the hallway to the exit.

13.

'I'll have to buy new suspenders, garters and knickers for Jill. In the heat of passion, I ripped the ones she had on.'

Skipper spoke as he and Albert made their way towards Eve and Jill's flat in Rathmines.

Albert stopped to turn back. 'I'm not going up there with you, you'll embarrass me. What's she going to think if she hears you talking like that?'

'Like what? I'm only telling you what happened.'

'I'm not going up. What am I going to say to her – that I was just passing?'

'She called to your flat, didn't she? Tell her you were lying down and you couldn't sleep; you were too sex starved. I'm only kidding. I promise I won't say anything that may mar your chances of a good night.'

'Skipper, you're not to say anything at all to her.'

'I promise I won't say a word to her. She's a nice girl. Mind you, not as nice as Jill if you know what I mean.'

He would have to trust Skipper yet again. He had not the courage to call alone. The thought of seeing her quickened his blood. He was drunk the last time he saw her. Was she really as beautiful as he remembered? He blushed as he recalled asking her how much she charged.

Jill answered the door as if she was expecting Skipper. She was all dressed up, with a wide smile.

She looked over at Albert. 'Skipper told me you had your eyes clamped on Eve. I'd say she'll be pleased. You look good.'

'You too, Jill.'

'She's in her room, I think. Do you want to knock on her door?'

'Would you mind asking her will she come out to me?'

'Sure.'

'Am I going to be left here, standing in the cold?' said Skipper. 'Or am I to be invited in?'

'Come on in Skipper. Good luck Albert, catch you later.'

He pulled the hood of his duffel coat as an Autumn mist drifted across the doorway. Then, as he looked out at the haze, he heard her dulcet voice.

'Come in! Surely Jill asked you in?'

He looked at her. Her long black hair blew over her face with the wind. She brushed it to the side. He would never be drunk again, for now in his sober state he was overawed with her smile.

'Jill did ask me in, but I thought I'd better wait until I saw you.'

'It's okay. Come on in. I was just about to make a cup of tea.'

She led him to her room and he sat down. He was cautiously trying to think of something to say, something that might impress her. His efforts were fruitless; for although he saw poetry in her every move, he could not find the words to express his feelings. Besides, he did not know her, and she was aware of his meeting with Jill. She moved gracefully around the room, busily making the tea. He got a poignant smell of incense, which was coming from a stick hanging out of a bowl on the mantelpiece. A wooden cuckoo sang and popped out to remind them it was ten o'clock.

'I burn incense when I'm smoking pot in the event of a police raid. They find it more difficult to establish you're smoking. Right now I'm a bit stoned. You get drunk, I get stoned. I get drunk too, sometimes. It's really nice to drink tea when you're stoned.'

'I never tried it.'

'It's okay. From what I know, it harms you no more than ordinary cigarettes. At least so I'm told. But sure we're going to die anyway.'

His thoughts were in an utmost state of confusion. My God, are there any normal people in Dublin? Albert wondered if Davey was a homosexual from the way he carried on with the Professor. Skipper was definitely a sex maniac from the way that he talked. Jill was a prostitute. And now Eve was a drug addict.

'Would you like to try one?'

'Yes.'

He was smitten. He would become a drug addict with her. She had him within her spell. He would do anything for her – just to be in her company. Her voice was so soft, ladylike; her dark brown eyes were worth dying for. She had a record sleeve on her lap, and was rolling this so-called joint. Every now and again she would look up at him with those alluring eyes.

'What happens when I take it? Do I go on a trip or something?'

'No. Nothing like that. You just relax. It may help to take your mind off other things. Here, you just inhale and hold it in your lungs for a while. Like so.'

She took a few pulls and then handed it to Albert. Albert puffed and inhaled again and again as Eve went to put on a record. It was Ann Byrne singing 'Come by the hill'. He felt weak, although he could hear the song with great clarity. He passed the joint back to her and was hoping she would not return it. But she did.

'Are you alright?'

'I think so.'

'Come on. Let's take a walk in the rain.'

She put on her coat and they walked out into the autumn night.

*

65

The rain had stopped. The wet pavement had a mirror effect, reflecting the moon and the neon lights from the shops. He felt light on his feet as though he was floating, and every sound their shoes made as they waded along the wet sidewalk was strangely clear; clearer than any sound he had ever noticed before. He wanted to take her hand, but was afraid she might refuse and think him silly. They walked down by the canal. A barge carrying merchandise was passing. She shouted to the man on deck for a lift to the next bridge. He smiled at her indubitable beauty and at the melodious voice that could know no refusal.

They stood on the deck and watched the colours of the street lights dancing around their reflections in the water.

'I'm going to buy one of these one day Albert, and I'm going to live in it. I'm going to go through all those lovely country villages, read all the poetry, and look at all that wild scenery. Yes, that's me.'

When they got home, they stopped at the door. He was only a foot away from her, and almost able to smell the sweet scent of her breath. Could he scrape up the courage to kiss her? His heart was beating fast and she knew it. They could hear Skipper and Jill in the other room. He leaned forward.

'Enough of this auld kissing Jill, and off with the knickers.'

Albert pulled away with embarrassment and Eve gave a laugh, once again putting her childlike hand to her mouth.

'Good night, Eve.'

'Good night, Albert. Do call again.'

*

As he walked home towards Leeson Street, he sang to himself.

Come by the hills, to the land where fancy is free,

And stand where the sea meets the sky, and the lough meets the sea.

66

Where the river runs free, and the bracken is gold in the sun.
And where cares of tomorrow must wait, till this day is done.

*

Albert became conscious of footsteps behind him as he approached Leeson Street. He didn't look back, but quickened his step. As he moved faster, so did the steps following him. He approached the hall door.

'I've been looking for you,' said a voice. 'The name is Dale Young. I'd like to come in and have a word with you.'

Albert turned around. Yes, he recognised him. He was the man he saw in the Pembroke at the back of the bar when Skipper had interrupted himself and Jill. He froze.

'I don't know you. What do you want?'

'You will know me. When we go in I'll tell you what I want.'

Albert was shaking as he opened the door. They headed upstairs.

'Nice place you've got here. I met your friend – what's this his name is?'

'I don't know. Which one do you mean?'

'The one I had a little problem with outside the Pembroke. If there's one thing that galls my blood, it's a smart fucker, and he's one of them. Unless he was too drunk. I gave him a little warning. Next time, I'll break his legs. You see, you've been messing around with one of my girls, Jill, and someone has to pay the price. It gets easier if I get it in cash, otherwise I have to get paid in pounds of flesh. Now I figure the former is more gentleman-like, and I take you for a gentleman.'

'What did I do? I never went near her.'

Albert was sitting down, while Dale paced up and down the room. He walked over to Albert and stood on his foot as he spoke.

'Don't fuck around with me, pal. How you pay me is your own

67

concern. I'll call next week, and for your own sake, for Jill's, and your mate, don't breath a word to them about this. Because should you, the consequences will be horrendous for whomever.'

He took out a big cigar and lit a match from the thigh of his trousers.

'I'll call next week. If I happen to meet you with any of your friends, just introduce me as your friend, Dale. As I said, don't fuck around with me. See you later.'

He turned and was gone, leaving the door ajar on his exit. Albert stood up, closed the door, and threw himself on the bed. The night wind whined through the open sash of his window. He thought of the relief he had felt when he heard the news from the doctor; how he had celebrated. This was worse than an infection. It was like the dentist telling him his teeth were alright, but the gums were all rotten. If only he had Eve by his side to tell him what to do. To share in his sorrow. As he thought of her, he realized he needed her more than anything. He was in love. A love that knows no fear, but the want of a true companion.

14.

Skipper never turned up for work for the rest of the week. Albert kept to himself and although there were numerous requests from Eamonn and Anthony as to whether something was the matter, he smiled and said no. He tried to be an island; alone and apart from others, like in the song.

When Saturday came, Albert strolled down town with his haversack on his back towards the bus for Donard. He was the first there, so he took the front seat upstairs on the double-decker.

Only two people had occupied his thoughts that week. Firstly, there was that evil looking one who called himself Dale. A cold shiver grasped his spine every time he thought of him. And then there was Eve – who gave him different sensations. He had not called to her that week though she was his only consoling comfort. The two figures were pulling at one another in his heart like heaven and hell, sanity and insanity.

The Saturday afternoon shoppers were busied about the town. Some of them are buying presents for their loved ones, he thought as he gazed out through the window. Why had Jill failed to tell him of the consequences of going out with her? He had never imagined that she would bring a gold digger into his life; a thug who could only be defied at the expense of someone's health. He could not even discuss it with her or Skipper. The bus was beginning to fill up now and the driver had started the motor. He closed his eyes as the bus drove away. His thoughts slipped into the oblivion of sleep. It was a relief from his hurt.

'I'd say the best thing about Dublin is the road to Donard and the best thing about Donard is the road to the Glen.'

Skipper sat himself down beside Albert, who started as he woke up.

'Here, I have an envelope for you. It's that few bob we agreed on Larry's horse. I hope I wasn't missed in work, I've been on the gargle. Wait till I tell you – that Jill is some tulip. Do you know what she did?'

'Don't tell me. Keep your voice down, Skipper.'

'She want's me to marry her. You can't trust them. And your one Eve's not to be trusted either. You couldn't be up to them.'

'What are you talking about?'

'Isn't she going with Davey?'

'Davey?'

'Aren't the two of them sitting behind in the bus? Did you not know?'

'What are you talking about?'

'I thought you knew – that's why you were sitting so far apart?'

Albert looked around and saw Eve and Davey sitting beside one another at the back of the bus. Eve waved and gave a smile of felicity, and Davey nodded. Lightning loaded with jealously shot through Albert's body. There was a difficulty with his breathing and it became an effort. My very best friend with the one I love, he thought. He had known Davey for so long and was trying to protect him from the Professor. Davey could not have done something like that to Albert. Was it that he had done bad things and now bad things were happening to him? Was the Lord taking it out on him on this very earth for his sins? My God! Jill! He had not gone to confession! In fact he had not even prayed. Dale was the Devil, coming to collect his debts. Rain was falling now on the window of the bus. It bounced like hailstones on the glass. Pellets from hell. Skipper must have seen the panic in his face for he was uncharacteristically silent. Could he jump in front of the bus through the glass window and end his misery?

'I didn't even know Davey knew her,' Albert said. 'It shows you, never trust the quiet ones.'

Beads of perspiration hung from his forehead like the dawn dew on a mountain. They were all singing on the bus now, 'The banks of the Ohio'. It sounded like a lament for the dead.

*

When the bus reached Donard, Albert was the last off. Skipper, Davey and Eve were standing on the pavement. He neither stopped nor looked towards them, but headed to Moynihan's Pub.

He stood at the corner of the small bar, trying to pull himself together. Skipper, Davey and Eve came in. Skipper was laughing, which added pain to Albert's labouring thoughts.

'Go tell him, Davey,' Skipper said.

Davey and Eve walked towards Albert.

'I had to bring her, Albert,' Davey said. 'She kept on asking me.'

Albert looked around at Davey. He knew he would be fighting a losing battle when he looked at his friend's face for it was a jewel of male perfection.

'We've five nights of the week for women,' said Skipper, 'and the last two days in the mountains are for the men. Mind you – you'd need a rest after five nights with them. I would anyway, after Jill.'

'This is my sister, Eve,' said Davey. 'She told me on the bus she knew you.'

Eve lifted her dark eyebrows, as she spoke. 'Don't be angry

Albert. I came out to take some photographs.'

How childish and foolish he felt. They knew the moods he had shown against them. Although his heartbeat softened from fury to excitement, he could not smile. It would have looked false and brought a tear to his eye. She smiled, and in a playful shy way turned her eyes towards the ground. It told him that he meant something to her. They hit a special chord when their eyes met. She had taken the bait he had thrown, and lowered that protective defence females inherit.

'Is there anybody buying a drink, for fuck's sake?' said Skipper. 'Albert, you have a face on you there like a bulldog licking piss off a nettle.'

All laughed, and Albert smiled at last.

'Two pints,' he said. 'And what would you like, Eve?'

15.

Cotton-wool clouds floated like helium balloons across the grey and azure sky of the Autumn evening. The rain had made the road a glossy black and had darkened the leaves on the ground and the green grass in the fields. Skipper and Davey walked ahead while Eve and Albert followed.

'I hope you're not sorry I came?' said Eve.

'I'm glad!'

'Where are you staying?'

'Probably in a shack called Stranahealy,' said Albert. 'And you?'

'In the hostel in Ballinclea.'

'That's only another half a mile down the road.'

'Davey said he would stay there too,' said Eve.

'You will come down to Fenton's and sing us a song?'

'I will.'

She had taken his hand. It was ladylike, fragile, and fitted exactly into his. He was not very tactical when she asked where he was staying; he should have said he had not made up his mind. She pressed his hand and stopped as if stepping on the brakes in a motor.

'Look Albert! The mountains are covered with a light mist! I've never seen that before. Are they violet?'

As he looked at her, her face lit into ecstasy. She wore a band around her forehead, and the light of the moon shadowed the features on her face. Being here with her was the nearest thing to paradise he could have imagined. Would he, before the night was out, get a chance or have the courage to kiss her?

*

'Do you know what I'm going to tell you, Mrs Fenton?'

'I have an idea, Skipper. And I'm on your side when we get a game of cards going.'

'You're the prettiest person I've seen. If you weren't married and I wasn't married we'd be the perfect couple. Maureen O'Hara hasn't a patch on you.'

'I don't know about that, Skipper. I don't think I'd be able to keep tabs on you. I think you're a bit of a fly-by-night. Wouldn't you say so, Albert? Why don't you bring the missus out here and let's have a good look at her? We could tell her a few home truths.'

'She's where she belongs, in the kitchen with the worn slippers.'

Albert, Eve and Davey sat down across from the bar while Skipper went to play darts with the locals.

'How come, Davey, you never told me about this place?' said Eve.

'I never see you much these days.'

'How did yourself and Davey meet?' she said to Albert.

'We meet in the youth hostel in Valencia, beside Cahirsiveen, a few years ago. Didn't we, Davey?'

'Yeah. We must go back there someday.'

Albert suddenly became apprehensive as he realised that he had lied to Eve about his age. In further conversation it was sure to come out. He was considerably younger than Eve. He wanted to be more attached to her before he told her the truth. He would try to get her on her own and walk and talk with her.

'Let's all play a game of darts.' Albert stood up as he spoke.

Skipper was already playing as they got to the board.

Albert went up to Davey who was at the bar. 'Davey, will you do something for me?'

'Of course. What's that?'

'Please don't tell Eve what age I am.'

'She's not stupid, Albert. She already knows that.'

Albert pulled back with a sudden jerk and looked over at Eve. She caught his eye and smiled. Did she know all along that Albert was a friend of her brother's? Was he fooling himself, thinking of her as a potential lover? Maybe a friend was all she wanted to be, a companion. It was more than a coincidence that Davey and herself were brother and sister. Perhaps she had known all along? They certainly would have discussed Albert on the bus to Donard. His heart paced faster. But if that was the case, then why did she take his hand as they walked to the pub?

He walked over to her, briskly. 'I'm going to stay in the hostel tonight as well.'

*

'What are you doing, Donie? Are you my partner or not? It's fucking marbles you should be playing.'

'It's a kick in the marbles you should be getting, Skipper. Look I'm after getting a double five. That's you gone, Mrs Fenton.'

'That was a fluke, Donie,' said Skipper. 'Don't buy a sweep ticket, you'll find one.'

'Ah, go and ask the butt end of me bollix, Skipper.'

'Ah, come on boys. Cut down on the language.'

'He's not the full shilling, Mrs Fenton,' said Skipper. 'Keep taking the tablets, Donie. They're keeping you reasonably stable.'

'They must be, because who scored for Francis's last Saturday, Skipper? Yeah, Donie did. Let me hear you say it?'

'Sure football is not a game at all. That's only for children.'

75

Skipper, Morris, Mrs Fenton and Donie had sat down. Eve, Albert and Davey sat beside them, with Albert opposite Eve and as close as was possible. He wanted to have as much of her beauty as he could within his sight.

Skipper continued. 'What's the point of running around a field getting all sweated up over a leather ball? Then supposedly adult men kiss one another when they get it in between two poles? Sure that's a queer's game.'

'Fuck off, Skipper. I'm no pig's ear.'

'Rugby, now that's a man's game,' Maurice said.

'They're only posh fellas taking it out on one another,' said Skipper. 'Do you know when they get down for a scrum and you can't see what their doing? They're all loafing one another! See all the bandages around their heads? Now, hurling seems to have a bit of skill. Who founded that, now? Cú Chulainn. Weren't we told in school that he hit a ball with a stick in Tyrone and ran and caught it in Limerick before it fell? Those teachers must have thought we were right gobshites. I think that was the time Saint Patrick was chasing the snakes out of Ireland.' Skipper paused. 'Did you hear about the fella who was playing golf with Donie's mot? He wore two pairs of trousers in case he got his hole in one.'

'You say fuck-all about my Nancy!'

'Do you remember years ago, we used to buy nancy balls, aniseed balls? Well that was Donie's nickname. Nancy used to work in a grocery store and Donie was always going in, throwing his eye on her. The same way Albert is throwing his eye on Eve. So all the kids used to call Donie, Nancy's balls.'

Eve was smiling. The dim light in the bar shadowed the curves of the features of her face. Albert could not take his eyes from her. He had tried – so it would not look so noticeable to the onlookers. But when he turned away, even for an instant, his eyes would return to her beauty by themselves.

Mrs Fenton came over brandishing a whiskey in one hand and

a cigarette in the other. 'Is there anyone going to sing?'

'We have a new singer here, Mrs Fenton. Albert's mot, Eve.'

'God then Skipper, you'll never find a girl as pretty as her.'

Eve sang 'Believe Me if All Those Endearing Young Charms'. Her eyes closed and she became engrossed in her task. The sound of her voice singing sad love ballads with melancholy airs would make Caruso sound as though he was singing out of key, Albert thought. If ever waves of minims and crotchets circled the air with purity and found a welcoming home, Eve's song found one in Albert's ears and in his heart. Skipper had told Mrs Fenton aloud she was Albert's girlfriend, and Eve had not retaliated in any form. She had not reacted at all.

*

There was a moonlit sky as the crimson sunset ebbed away like the lava of a volcano. Some candyfloss clouds sailed overhead. Skipper and Davey were walking ahead of them. Albert took another step in wooing by putting his left hand around her waist. It was as though they were made for each other. Her hand slid smoothly into his like a glove.

'Each time I come out her there are sunsets with different colours. It would be impossible to even try to explain them to anybody at home.'

'It's hard to believe it's autumn, Albert. When you think of the talents we're given from above. Some can sing, paint, write poetry. Different talents for different people. Yet the one beauty He has given to all who can see and hear is nature and its sunsets.'

He brought her to a halt with his hand and turned her towards him. The moonlight had made a perfect silhouette of her childlike face and her girlish grin. He kissed her and his lips found the perfect kiss. His heart was beating rapidly, as was hers. An owl hooted from the forest behind them as though apologizing for its intrusion, and the rest of the forest wildlife seemed to rustle excitedly at their Romeo and Juliet. With all the heavenly pastoral powers, it was a fairyland setting.

'I'm too old for you, Albert.'

She was whispering through heavy breathing.

'You're not. But anyway, I wouldn't care.'

'I think we should go on to the hostel before we do what we might regret. When I tell you about myself, you'll change your mind.'

'You needn't tell me; I know you're a drug addict and I don't care.'

She pulled away and gave the warmest laugh Albert had seen, causing him to laugh as well.

'I'm no drug addict, although I'm mad enough to be one!'

They laughed and talked of nature as they strolled through the russet leaves towards the hostel.

16

'Anything strange or startling, Eamonn?'

Mr Broderick had walked into the main office. He stood swivelling on the balls of his feet as he spoke, as if poised at the edge of a cliff contemplating suicide.

'The weather's strange for autumn and I would imagine the rises in January will be startling.'

Mr Broderick ignored the remark as his creative thoughts, if he had any, were in limbo.

'Did you start Albert on the wages yet?'

'Today, Mr Broderick.'

'Pay attention then, Albert. You tend to be a bit sleepy. I check and sign them in the afternoon.'

'Yes, Mr Broderick, Sir.'

Eamonn's phone rang and he answered.

'I'm afraid that was bad news,' he said. 'Peader has passed away.'

'We better get someone down to Bond Road to take his place,' said Mr Broderick.

Passed away, Albert thought to himself. Does that mean he's dead? Beads of perspiration formed on his forehead. He had never thought of death, and never known someone close to die. Here he was, trying to fulfil his own lustful desires with Jill and now with Eve, and the almighty hand above had the power to call him for inspection at any minute. From his record he would be doomed forever. He would go straight to hell. Could he get to confession fast enough to tell and ask forgiveness for himself and Jill? The teacher in school said that if we sinned in life on earth, the good Lord would forgive us even at the last moment. More perspiration ran down his back as he thought of himself as a cowardly hypocrite.

'I've just been on the phone to Peader's daughter,' said Eamonn. 'He died last night and his wake will take place in his house this evening. Will you come, Albert? I know his daughter, she's a school teacher. She's taking it alright.'

*

A sombre ghostly feeling fumigated the air as Albert, Eamonn and Anthony entered Peader's house. The was a smell of death. Skipper was sitting in the corner of a crowded kitchen. Save for Albert's companions, Skipper was the only other person Albert knew at the wake. People wore black, the colour of death. Their faces were pale and ghastly.

'Noreen,' said Eamonn. 'A sad day for a great character. The end of an era. I spoke to you on the phone and I met you before.' He extended his hand, and then introduced her to Albert and Anthony.

'Would you like a drink?' she said. 'There's room in the sitting room. He's stretched out in the bedroom.'

'I'll look after them, Noreen,' Skipper said. 'What'll you have, lads?' He stood up and made his way to get the drinks. 'Go on into the front room and I'll bring yous in the drinks.'

Two teachers sat at either end of the couch, and a third on an easy chair. Albert, Eamonn and Anthony sat on chairs that were leaning against the wall. Skipper came in with drinks, and then left to answer the hall door. When Noreen took over the greeting of the new mourner, Skipper returned to the sitting room.

'We're graced with the local constable. None less important

80

than our own Larry.'

Larry was well tanked with alcohol. He staggered through the sitting room door and panned his eyes around the room, finally settling them on a bottle of whiskey which was on a coffee table adjacent to the far wall. He headed towards it with remarkable alacrity lest someone get there before him. 'Auld Peader had good innings,' he said. With the whiskey in his left hand, he observed a vacant space between the two young schoolteachers on the couch and he made his way towards the cleft. Without using the springs on the hinges of his knees, he let fly his enormous buttocks into the gap, wedging himself between the pair and cracking the butt of the whiskey bottle on the young teacher's knee.

The teacher made horrendous efforts at withstanding the pain without notice.

'I knew auld Peader years ago,' said Larry. 'He used to keep greyhounds. He had a few fair bitches.'

'He was a good age,' Eamonn said.

'He was in me bollix. My auld lad's ninety-three and he's after booking his holidays in Butlin's for next year. Keeps telling us he can't wait for the roller-coaster. For fuck's sake, I never noticed you there Darren. Are you still teaching? It's a small fucking world. Do you know me? Larry Coyne, I'm in the guards. Do you remember fucking years ago we used to play cards? You must fucking remember.'

'To my regret. I observe you've lost none of your kindness or finesse.'

'Thanks very much Darren. You were always a class bloke.'

The young teacher sitting beside the guard forced his way out of the lock on the couch, stood up and limped into the other room. Albert also got up, and made his way up the stairs to the toilet. A ghostly silence hung on the air of the upper floor, and only when leaving the toilet did he realize why. In the bedroom, he caught sight of Peader's open coffin. He walked towards the room like a frightened child. Save for the dead corpse, the room was empty. Peader lay with his hands crossed and rosary beads on same. He had a false smile on his jaundiced wax face. Albert was speechless.

He suddenly felt as though everybody else in the house had left. He tried to move, but could not. Then he thought he saw the corpse move. There were screams of laughter from above in his mind. It was the devil laughing at him, mocking him.

The devil spoke and put his hand on his shoulder.

'I'd say he's a model for your man above. I mean he led a simple enough life. Are you coming over to see Eve and Jill?'

Skipper was standing beside Albert. The spirit re-entered Albert's body, and he felt like grabbing Skipper for a crutch. But he hesitated, lest the Judge above might think he was taking the side of the devil.

'Not now. Maybe later.' Albert's confused body brushed Skipper aside and fumbled his way down the stairs. Without looking into the sitting room, he opened the front door and went out to the fresh air.

*

The night was as black as death itself, and as he walked briskly he shivered.

He caught a bus into town, and as he walked the aisle he became conscious that everyone was staring at him. It was as though they were informed of his sins. When he had taken a seat upstairs, he saw that the rain had started heavily and was pounding on the glass. Alarmed, he pulled away from the window and sat on the outside of the seat. He closed his eyes and was only waiting for thunder and lighting to strike, to catch the bus and blow it into oblivion.

*

Albert got off the bus in Dame Street and walked around Georges Street up to Whitefriar Street Church. His anorak and trousers were a wet sponge and weighed heavily like his sins. The church's sombre shade of light mixed with the smell of incense. A melancholy drone echoed softly around the church from a practising organist. He looked towards the confession box, and could see the dim light shining overhead. There were two elderly people kneeling outside, waiting to go in. An old women exited the box now, blessing herself, and the next person went in. He tried to gather his thoughts and looked up at the statue of the Lord. The statue was looking at him with a warm forgiving look on its face. He suddenly thought of Peader, and he realised how selfishly worried he was being about his own demise. The Lord had given him time to repent. Peader had no say in the matter.

He tried to say as many prayers as possible to get up the courage to go in. The last person had entered the box.

When his turn came, he stood up and moved down the aisle, his legs accelerating with every step. His wet shoes gave a squelching sound which echoed around the church. It must have set the organist astray, for she stopped. He felt he was on display. The old lady who had left the confession box had knelt down and was facing him. As he approached, the light went out and the priest emerged, almost accidently hitting him with the door. The gates of heaven had closed on him, he thought.

'A wet evening, my child?'

Having spoken, the priest put his hand on his shoulder. The organ had started up again and the old woman was coughing.

'Are the confessions finished Father?'

'There always time in the house of God, my child. Come in.'

The cleric would be sorry he had put his hand on his shoulder when he heard what Albert had to tell him. He felt certain the man thought he had found a new recruit for the priesthood by the way

83

he had looked at him. There was a gentle cough and the shutter opened. He could see the darkened silhouette through the wire gauze. As he spoke he watched the heavenly look on the shadowed features. When he would reveal all, that face would look towards him, the penny would drop, and his welcoming smile would turn to a scowl.

When he came to telling the priest about smoking marijuana, he was taken aback when the silhouette asked in a pleasant voice what it felt like. Albert knew that he would never be a recruit for the priesthood, but he hoped he had not found a new recruit for marijuana.

The priest gave Albert a light penance. Albert wondered if this was because he had had the courage to reveal all? Or perhaps the man was just in a hurry home and wanted to close the church?

As he knelt down to say his penance, he felt as though a sack of rocks was lifted from his shoulders. Vapours of mist came from his clothes in the heat of the church, making their way towards the rafters high above. The priest passed him and smiled, bidding him goodnight.

The angels of heaven were singing in his ears as he left, welcoming their prodigal son back into the flock. He felt light on his feet as he walked, as though he had smoked marijuana; although he dared not think about such misdemeanours. The rain had stopped and the night showed the moon and a thousand stars. A gentle breeze tossed his hair. He thought it might be an angel placing a halo on his head.

When he got home, he made tea and went to bed. If he died in his flat this night, he would be in paradise. Pleasant thoughts turned to pleasant dreams as he felt welcomed back into God's kingdom. He floated into a deep sleep.

17.

Albert spent a couple of nights in holy bliss with the angels, praying as often as he could and avoiding Skipper like the plague. In his dreams at night he sat on the clouds with the other angels, drinking plonk and discussing how the weather was always perfect. Eve was one of the heavenly reincarnations around him, but she was a constant taxation to his mind. She always sat on a cloud opposite him, smiling. Everything seemed perfect until Albert noticed the agonising rattle of false teeth. He looked around at all the other angels and realised that they were old, over eighty, and that it was their false teeth that sounded as they ate and drank.

He would suddenly wake, and Eve would be all that was left in his mind. To distract himself, he would pray with remarkable fervour.

He came to the realization that he was becoming a saint sixty years before all these other angels.

Anyway, he had done nothing wrong with Eve – save for the kiss he gave her.

*

'Eve wants to know if she can come away with us next weekend? She said she really enjoyed the Glen. She was expecting you to call over.'

Davey was sitting beside Albert in the Chinaman.

'I'd love her to come. I'm going to call over to her tonight.'

'Do you want a drink?'

'A lemonade. I'm going to give my stomach a rest.'

'I think I'll take your advice and try the same.'

'How come you never told me Eve was your sister?'

'How was I supposed to know you knew her? I haven't seen much of her since childhood. We were fostered by different people.'

'You mean she wasn't raised by those people I met you with when I was in Cahirciveen?'

'No. They're the people that fostered me when I was only three. Their name is Chapman. Eve was brought up by a family by the name of Robertson.'

'What happened to your own family?'

'They were killed in a fire accident when I was only three. I don't remember them that well. Eve sometimes tells me about them. She was ten.' Davey took a swig of lemonade. 'Do you know that Eve was married and has a five year old daughter?'

Albert opened his mouth without saying anything for a long time. He was trying to find some words to match his thoughts when he heard a familiar voice.

'Have I leprosy or something? I get the impression somebody's avoiding me. What are you two having? I cut a right hole in that few pounds I won. What are you having Albert? You look like a pioneer sitting down there.'

Davey winked at Albert as Skipper joined the company. Their conversation would have to be put on hold for a later date.

'We're only drinking lemonade, Skipper.'

'Lemonade me bollix. Barman? Give us three pints. I see the builders' strike is going ahead.'

'It won't effect us Skipper.'

'Of course it will effect us. By the way I'm sorry for giving out about bringing women away with us for the weekends to the Glen. On reflection, I think it's a great idea. I asked Jill to come next weekend. It would be a good place to rehearse the play. It's about time we got started. There's a good lot of work to be done on it and there's no harm in mixing work and pleasure.'

'Yeah, well my sister wants to come too.'

'Could we get Davey fixed up with a bird, Albert? Surely Jill has plenty of mates. Have you any money Dave, and you'll be promised a good time? Right Albert? Tell him.'

'I'm alright the way I am for the moment, Skipper.'

'You can't go on pumping the bike for the rest of your life Davey. If you are looking for one, be careful! Choose a big dumb blonde that has a pub beside a bookie shop.'

'Don't listen to him, Davey. He'll set your mind astray.'

Skipper went on fool-acting with Davey. Albert pretended to listen, but his mind was elsewhere. Davey had never talked much about anything, let alone about himself. Albert pondered on what Davey had told him about his sister being married and about his family. He had at times noticed a sadness in his friend's eyes, but never asked about it. Davey was a deep thinker. A vision came to his mind now of the times they walked the hills together. Often, for no apparent reason, Davey would stop and sigh. Long silences were normal with Davey. Albert had never asked why; he did not want to be an intruder in his mind. Now, he understood; the pieces of the youth's puzzle were falling into place. Davey was a loner. A lump heaved in Albert throat when he thought of how much a stranger he had been to his best friend.

'Who's buying a gargle for me, for fucks sake?'

'I'll buy you one Skipper, because we're going.'

'Where are you two off to? Wait till I have a couple more gargles, and I'll go up as far as Jill and Eve with you. By the way, Jill said Eve wanted to see you.'

*

87

Later, they were alone again.

'Come back to my flat, Davey. We'll get something to eat.'

'Yeah. I might as well.'

Twilight was drawing its coat over Dublin City as the youths leisurely walked towards Albert's flat. As they approached Leeson Street there was a young man sitting on the corner, drinking a bottle of wine.

'I know you, don't I?' the man said. 'We had a drink the other day with Terry. Don't you remember?'

'I do,' said Albert. 'Look, here's ten shillings.'

It was the toucher Nelson.

'No,' he said. 'I'm not looking for money. You see, I'm on the street four years now and all that time my dog was by my side. I slept around there in the archway in Pembroke Street last night, and when I woke my dog was gone. I haven't seen him since. He means more to me than all the money anybody could give.'

'He'll come back.'

'I'd hate to think he was knocked down or that.'

A dog is a man's best friend, Albert thought. He looked into the vagabond's sad eyes, detected a tear, and was startled that even the worn and the wild had feelings and compassion. He spoke well and Albert wondered why he had not walked the straight line of life, but fell below it for whatever reason.

'Why don't you try the Garda station? Some people do report stray dogs.'

'The Garda station?'

'Sure. There's no harm in trying.'

'They wouldn't listen to me.'

'Come on, we'll go over to Kevin Street with you.'

*

'Ah, for fuck's sake toucher, go on down to the Iveagh Hostel.

You're not fucking sleeping here. Don't tell me yous two have taken to the street?'

Larry was speaking with his mouth full of a vulgar sandwich and a gigantic mug of tea in his right hand.

'His dog is missing.'

'His dog? What the fuck do you think this is – the RSPCA?'

'Ah no, Larry. He's a black collie. He was an expensive dog. I bought him from a sheep farmer.'

'We're asked to look after robberies, even to watch fuckers going around with no lights on their bikes. I'm dying with a hangover, and you're asking about a tramp's dog? Give us a break, for fuck's sake.'

'He's only asking about an expensive dog.'

'Did anybody see a dog that swallowed a television? No. Now fuck off, toucher.'

They felt sad for Nelson as they left the station.

'Here, take this – ten shillings. It might bring you luck, and we're sure you'll find him.'

*

Davey was sitting on the couch, using his arm as an arch to prop up his chin. Albert wondered about what Davey had told him as he made tea. 'And you tell me Eve was married and has a daughter?'

'Yeah. Didn't she tell you? You better not start questioning me about her. I thought you knew. I don't want to get in trouble, especially with women. You best ask herself about it.'

'I had no idea that the two of you were orphans, let alone brother and sister. How come you were brought up by two different families?'

'There wasn't a lot of work and everybody seemed to have big families. Those people that took me, their name was Chapman. I can tell you they were some family. Dessie Chapman, he was from Cahirsiveen in Co. Kerry. He treated me like a son. He was a member of the Kerry mountain rescue squad. He brought me over all those mountains, the McGillicuddy Reeks, Carrauntoohil and every other mountain in Kerry. He read me all those stories about the great explorers, Scott, Amundsen, Shackleton, Harrer, Hillary and the rest. I was mesmerized by those stories. Men measuring their strengths against mysterious landscapes. Hillary was always my favourite.'

'Who got there first, Davey? To the top of Everest.'

'It seems to be one of the secrets. Over in this part of world, we were always told Hillary. And in Tibet, I suppose they were always told Tensing.'

'And who do you think?'

'I don't know. But Dessie was always of the opinion it was Hillary, because he had the experience to climb those last icy cliffs.'

'Is he still alive?'

'Hillary, yeah.'

'I know that. I'm talking about Dessie.'

'He is, yeah. He retired from work, last year. Moved back down to his hometown. You must come down with me some day.'

'I'd like to.'

The ringing of the doorbell interrupted them and Albert made his way to answer it.

It was Dale. He wore a pin-stripped suit and looked even more devious than before. 'Albert, glad to find you in. I believe you were looking for me.'

'What do you want? How much do you want?'

'Well now. Let's start by asking how much you earn?'

'Look, I don't go with Jill.'

'Are you telling me I'm imagining things, seeing you and that other headbanger going in and out of where she lives? I mean

90

don't fuck around with me. If you tell me it's the other bloke, then I'll break his fucking limbs. Or both your fucking limbs. So what's it going to be?'

'Eight pounds seventeen shillings a week.'

'You want to keep out of trouble by giving me eight pounds seventeen shillings a week?'

'That's what I earn.'

'Look, I'm a reasonable bloke. I'll keep your head above water for five pounds. And a little payment now would be appreciated.'

'I have to go upstairs. Will you wait here? I have a mate of mine upstairs.'

'Don't keep me waiting long. I get impatient very easy.'

'I can imagine.'

Albert made his way upstairs. When he re-entered the room, Davey was sitting rigidly on the couch. He must have seen the alertness in Albert's eyes, for he asked if Albert was okay. Albert went to where he kept the money in the wardrobe. It was the money he won on Larry's horse. Then he hastened his way back to the front door to Dale.

'For how long do I have to pay you?'

'I don't know, Albert. For how long do you want to live?' He gave a sardonic smile, turned and was gone.

Albert knew he had enough money to carry him for a couple of weeks, and then he would have to think what he would do after that. Davey had come to the door to see if all was well. He had his coat on, and he told Albert he would see him at the weekend.

18.

The clock cards were six inches by three. They were stamped on the front to indicate hours worked overtime, with a second stamp to indicate tax and insurance. Eamonn had gone over the details of what had to be done. When Albert finished the job, he asked Eamonn to give them a thorough examination and to correct any mistakes that might come to his view. Afterwards, Albert turned over the clock cards and carefully looked at same, wondering if there was a way he could embezzle finances to keep his unwelcome companion Dale at bay. The thought of going through life without a God-given limb did not appeal to him, not to mention having the arduous task of constantly explaining how he lost it. While pondering on this, he heard Mr Broderick's door opening with his signalling cough. He did his Captain Bligh walk and wedged himself between Eamonn and Albert.

'Anything strange or startling, Eamonn?'

'I hear the builders are gone out on strike. That will have a big effect on us.'

Mr Broderick raised his game now from slow pocket billiards to Japanese ping-pong tennis, using the keys in his pocket as a serving bat. It sounded like an alarm to Albert, which was upsetting, considering his earlier thoughts.

'We have to work all that harder. We may have to let people go if things don't pick up. We'll have to be on the ball, Eamonn.'

You're on the balls yourself Mr Broderick, Eamonn thought smiling to himself.

'Something funny, Eamonn?'

'I was just looking over at Albert, and admiring how well he did the wages for the first week. A bright lad!'

Mr Broderick coughed again, and took the handkerchief from his pocket to remove the spittle from his mouth. 'I'll sign them so.'

He turned and went back into his office. Albert followed, and as he got up his hair touched the sunlight. He felt it was the angel taking back his halo. Anthony, on the way to his hole to feed his habit, gave a contorted smile as he passed him.

Peader came to Albert's mind when he entered Mr Broderick's office, for it looked and smelt like a morgue. Mr Broderick was sitting down. It was the first aerial view he had got of him. It resembled a fried egg on top of a black mop. As he was signing, he suddenly stopped and looked up at Albert. His eyes had left their sockets, like a bullfrog eyeing prey.

'Two hours overtime?'

'One of the lorry drivers, Mr Broderick.'

Mr Broderick let fly a command. 'Anthony! Anthony!'

Anthony entered the office and opened his mouth. 'Yes?'

The fumes of the nicotine spread into the stagnant air of the office. Albert was about to thank God he was not in Anthony's position, but then he thought better of it, realising his earlier intentions. Mr Broderick gave a cough in Anthony's direction, letting him know that it was clear that he had been in his hole.

'Two hours overtime, Anthony. What's this about?'

'One of the drivers had to go to Arklow, Mr Broderick.'

'We can't have this! We have to fit the working time into a working day. Times are not good, and it would be awkward explaining this at board level. We have a builder's strike in hand, and a strike for ourselves pending. Could he finish early one of the days?'

'We could try it, Mr Broderick.'

'Adjust that one so, Albert. I have to go out, I'll sign it later.'

With that, he was gone down to Georges Street for his coffee break, and Albert heaved a sigh of relief.

*

As Albert walked towards Eve's flat, he worked out the details of his misdemeanour. With the very birth of his resolution, he could feel the sin on his soul and the burden on his feet doubled as if a boulder was placed upon his shoulders.

He had been given the keys of the clocking clock because it broke down so often and the suppliers were repeatedly called to fix it. On their next visit, he would observe how the clock could be set to a certain time required. Should he be able to find a name common enough that could go through without notice, there would be plenty of times he would be alone and could clock in a card for a fictitious person.

He praised his evil mind when he saw a way to do it. It would be unwise to pick an adult, because they had to pay tax and stamps; and not only would he have to deal with the rapacious Mr Broderick, he would be leaving himself a target for the Revenue as well. A nipper under sixteen would be the answer. Now, Foley's carriers were consistently up and down with timbers, all day and everyday. There was common talk in the office regarding Foleys. His heart was ticking as quickly as the clocking clock did –when it worked. Foley. He lighted on the name as a perfect solution to his plight.

Crossing the road with his mind in purgatory, he barely heard the blast of a horn from a motorbike telling him to get out of the way or be killed. In shock, Albert realised that if he was going to play twenty-ones with the man above, he might as well be on the alert. After all, He held the trump card that could burst him at any given minute.

The devil was laughing at him now as he neared Eve's Flat. He thought of her beauty.

Well, I may as well be hung for a sheep as a lamb, he thought as he approached the gate.

*

In her flat she threw her arms around him and gave him a kiss more lustful than he previously thought possible from the opposite sex, moving her body towards his in the closest movement of sin he could have imagined.

He put his two hands on her ebony silk hair, taking hold of her head. 'You never told me you were married.'

She was taken aback by his question and, like ice poured into hot water, she cooled off and turned away. 'Did Davey tell you?'

'Yes.'

'I've nothing to hide. I was going to tell you. I didn't get an opportunity in the pub, and I didn't think it the right time when we were walking home. I'll tell you about it.'

'First, I want to ask you a favour.'

'A favour?'

'Yes.'

'I want you to move out of here.'

'In with you, do you mean? I'd have to know you a bit better first, and you to know me too.'

'No. It's not that. Do you know Jill is a prostitute, and she lives in the same house as you?'

'That's up to herself. She doesn't bring her clients into her flat.'

'But people could be watching you coming to and from the same house.'

'Do you know something I don't know, Albert? You have a worried look on your face. Has somebody being talking to you, telling you something Jill and myself should know? Tell me what's wrong, Albert.'

She had moved closer towards Albert with a renewed confidence. He looked into her exquisite dark brown eyes. He wanted to tell her of Dale, and the slippery slope he had fallen into to avoid trouble. She would understand.

He was trying to keep the worried look from his eyes. 'I can't tell you just now Eve. But I will tell you sometime if you leave.'

'Is it so important that you mean now?'

'Maybe not. But it would put my mind at ease.'

'And where could I go with such short notice?'

Albert turned away, wondering if suggesting that she could stay in his flat would make her think he was making strides towards winning her towards his heart – or his bed.

'You could stay in my flat until you can find a place of your own.'

'But you've only one bed.'

The blood rushed to Albert's face.

She looked at him and smiled. 'Of course – it's a double bed. How would I be able to bring over my things?'

'Get them ready and I'll get a taxi.'

Eve went to get her belongings with haste.

On the way out to get a taxi, Albert met Jill in the hall.

'Hi, Albert,' she said. 'Are you leaving?'

He was stuck for words until Eve appeared behind him.

'We're leaving, Jill. I'm moving in with Albert. We're in love. Aren't we Albert?'

Albert felt a lump in his throat and he felt sure he was about to choke.

'Why don't you go and get that taxi?' said Eve. 'And perhaps Jill will give me a hand to pack.'

It felt as though somebody had added yet another boulder to his shoulders as his knees wobbled their way down the Rathmines Road. He felt like Christian in the Pilgrim's Progress. His heart and pulse were beating like bongo drums at the prospect of living with Eve becoming a reality. She had reacted as though he had attacked her with his question about being married. He would have to aim for more success in his conversations with her or her brother in future. The thought that the true love of his life was coming to live with him made him smile. For he firmly believed it was true love he had found. He was down by the canal now, but there were still no taxis in sight.

*

'Don't worry about that, mum. You take that one, it's easy, and I'll get these into the cab.'

The taxi-man spoke as he picked up two suitcases, and surveyed half a room full of bags and paintings. He looked at her beauty with a broad smile on his face as he took off his coat and prepared for his labour. 'Just married, eh?'

'No. I'm just moving to Leeson Street.'

His broad smile turned to a frustrated, forlorn face. 'Leeson Street,' he said, tying the last knot of the rope to the roofrack.

*

Albert was filling the kettle while Eve was taking clothes out of her suitcase.

'Don't think I'm unpacking. I'll find a place tomorrow. I'm just getting my nightdress.' She girlishly put her hand to her face again and grinned. 'Or do I need it?

Albert was about to faint. Luckily for him, he had made it to the chair before she had spoken. If ever an aroma could be found to be an equal to the sweet flowers of nature, then Eve had found it. His room smelt like a bed of roses, and her face and features brought him closer to heaven than he had ever been before. Which

97

was just as well, he thought; because he was not siding with above.

She crossed him and put her nightdress under the pillow on the bed. He got up as the kettle had boiled, and handed her a cup of tea as he sat back down. 'I'll sleep on the couch.'

'Can I be that couch, Albert?'

There was an embarrassed pause from Albert, and Eve burst into laughter. A moment later he laughed also.

'Heck, Albert, let's smoke a joint.'

Albert looked on in amazement as Eve picked up a record sleeve and skilfully rolled a perfect joint, doing as fine a job as any craftsman applying his trade.

'Are you going to tell me why I would be in trouble if I stayed on in the flat?'

'I will Eve. But would you mind if I didn't tell you just now? I promise I'll tell you in the future.'

'Okay. Will you not ask me about my marriage, and I'll tell you in the future?'

*

They were smoking. Eve sat opposite him, and he could see her features even more clearly than before. When she spoke her voice was like crystal. Her voice was a summons to his heart.

'So Davey told you all about us?'

'No, not much. He told me you two were orphans, and you were brought up by a family by the name of Robertson.'

'Right. Yes, well they were good memories.'

'Tell me about them. About what they were like.'

'Oh, well, they were really nice people. They were unfortunate at the beginning, but they weathered the storm and came out great in the end.'

'How? How do you mean? What happened?'

'Well they came from a small place called Carrow. Well,

98

outside Carrow. His name's James. They're still alive. Her name is Eileen. Well apparently they fell in love a long time ago, and after a time courting, unbeknownst to any of the locals she became pregnant. Now at that time, that was a terrible thing to have to live with in the country, when you're not married. But they had even more complications. You see, they were first cousins. There wasn't much work around; he wasn't working, and with his situation there wasn't any prospect of his chances changing. So, with nobody's good cheers, they took off for England.

'He got a job on a building site, and she got a job cleaning in some sort of a café or the like. Well they were aware how difficult things were going to be, especially over here, because it was over here they wanted to live. So they saved and saved and eventually moved back with the hope of buying some land. They had their money, but there was no-one that would sell them any. They returned to England, and as things happened fortune did come their way. He got a better job when they were building a railway, and a neighbour in the digs they were staying in was also from Carrow. The other couple had emigrated many years previously and knew nothing about James and Eileens' situation. They were left land by an uncle, but they were happy there and had no intention of returning. So they sold the land to James and Eileen, with a small cottage.

'When they returned, they were made even less welcome. Their neighbours tried to intervene and protest over them acquiring the land, but their efforts were all in vain. They'd acquired it legally, and legally it was theirs. Well, they kept to themselves, and he did up the cottage and worked the farm although he had to go elsewhere to sell his wheat and grain. He had bought a second tractor and worked really hard. They had one child, Sineád, and despite the odds they were a great success. Eventually the past was all put behind them with the neighbours, and was only spoken about in whispers. They became bigger than most farmers around.

They were successful rebels to the community in that neighbourhood. I guess that's why I became a rebel to society. We learn as we get older.'

The joint was continually passed between them. Albert could feel himself floating in jewels of helium. Eve spoke with casual clarity, and the longer she spoke, the more drawn he was towards her. She could not possibly be twenty-four, for she had a child-like face which in no way carried the weight of years. He savoured the country twang in her voice, which she had inherited from James and Eileen. It was ringing in his ears, as it had when he heard the sound of her beautiful voice singing for the first time.

When she got up to make more tea, he watched with ecstasy as her body swayed in her light dress. 'And how did you fit in?' he asked, immediately blushing.

'I was treated just the same as one of their own, maybe even better. I think they were always conscious that I might have felt out of place, so they always held sway with me in any grievance. James played the accordion, and he sang all those real traditional songs. You know, in the real traditional manner. Of course we went to school over there, and his child went on to university. I could have gone, but I went to art college instead. In time we all move on, don't we? Well I moved on and got married and started my own life.' Eve stopped and touched her eye as if she was wiping a tear away. 'Well I nearly finished my own life. I'm only starting now.'

She got up and sat beside him; he put his arm around her and they started kissing. After a few minutes, they got into the double bed and a thousand more words were spoken in their bodies as they embarked on a magic carpet trip to paradise.

If this is what hell is like then it's where I want to be, Albert thought as he kissed her goodnight.

19

'I was reading in The Mirror yesterday that the average man thinks about sex every three minutes.'

Skipper, Jill, Albert, Eve, Davey and Donie were all sitting around the table in the Seskin Pub in the Glen.

'Well Skipper,' said Jill, 'you must be well above average.'

'I hope you weren't annoyed with me last night Jill, because I was brilliant.'

'Honest to God, Skipper, you're God's gift to women.'

Jill was wearing an unbelievably short mini-skirt. It was one of those mini-skirts that you wouldn't know where to look – but most men would, as was the case with all the local men in the pub.

'I couldn't be without you, Skipper. He's endowed with a piece of equipment that could only be compared to an ass's tail with a pig's heart.'

'You're boasting, Jill,' said Skipper. 'It's only like a baby's arm hanging out of a pram, holding an orange. Jill? Here's a fiver, go and get a couple of drinks, and rub off a couple of locals for the craic. Pretend you're flogging your mutton.'

'She is,' Donie said.

'Donie,' said Skipper, 'there's two oriental hostellers over there. See can you get off with one of them – and I'll give you a tenner if you can prove to me it's slanted.'

Albert was mortified, and even Davey looked embarrassed at the conversation in front of his sister. Eve had turned away, and was laughing at something that tickled her fancy.

'You could go nowhere with them,' Albert whispered to Eve and Davey. 'Skipper doesn't seem to care who he's talking to.'

'He doesn't mean it,' said Eve. 'It's all just frivolous fun. What's life without a laugh? There's too many serious people in the world.'

As Eve spoke, for the first time Albert could feel he was becoming jealous of her; was becoming possessive of her. He wanted to take her away on her own, to talk to her, listen to her, to get to know her better.

She spoke again, in a whisper. 'O Jesus look! Your woman is worse than Skipper.'

Jill was at the bar and had sandwiched herself between a couple of locals. She put her hand on one of their legs, right beside his arch. He froze solid like Saul.

Skipper stood up and was looking over at her and the unfortunate local – whom the locals thought was fortunate. 'I see Noel,' he said, 'you can still make an umbrella of your shirt. I don't mind yis pumping my wheels, as long as you know that it's me that's riding the bike.'

The local turned white and stood up, pulling his overcoat over his person and made his way to the toilet amidst a host of spectators.

'Ah, Skipper, you brought down the wife at last.'

'One of them, Mrs Fenton.'

'Is there anybody for cards?'

'Yes, we'll all play.'

Albert watched Eve as she talked, laughed and played cards. He watched the changing patterns in her face, from the joy of winning to a gentle sadness at losing. He was captivated by her, engrossed by every twitch of her face. He was hers and she was his.

102

'Ah, for fuck's sake Jill. How do you expect to walk up the mountains in high heels and a mini-skirt? Do you want to go down to the pub and wait for us?'

'I have an anorak. Is there no road up? I want to go, keep myself in shape. I need my body, you know.'

'I know you do – so do I need you body, Jill.'

'I'm wearing these boots, Jill,' said Eve. 'You can have these runners.'

They were at the foot of Cameragh Hill, as Eve took a pair of runners from her haversack. Skipper was going to lead them across the hills.

It was more like late summer than mid-autumn as they made their way up the mountain. Skipper was not pushing the pace, but rather sluggishly sauntered up the hill holding Jill by the hand. Albert held Eve's hand and Davey held her other hand. Albert felt there was a bond between the three of them; as if they were the only family that they or he had never known. The three were together as one. They reached the top of the first hill.

'I have to sit down, Skipper,' said Jill. 'My legs are exhausted.'

'O yes. Sit down, Jill. It wouldn't do for anything to happen to them.'

'Is this it?' she said. 'Do we turn back after this rest?'

'This is only the start, Jill. You see over there, that's Lug mountain. Well when we get there we'll walk right around the ring of the Glen, over Table and back into the Imaal in a couple of hours. A couple more week-ends like this, Jill, and you'll be fit for anything.'

Albert watched Eve and Jill as they made their way to the summit. He felt sorry for them, for fatigue was gaining the upper hand. He could see the sadness in Eve's eyes as she was brought to the limit of her physical endurance. The boys were well used to it, because of all the weekends they had walked the mountains. It was the girls' first time.

Sitting at the cairn was the Professor, shielding himself from the wind. He was smoking a pipe, and had a bottle of whiskey in one hand.

'Ah! My excellent young friends. Indeed I see you have brought some beautiful roses to the garden of paradise. I admire your taste. There is nothing more graceful to compliment our exciting scenery than the sight of two lovely females. Would anyone care for a drink?'

'How are you, Professor?'

Jill had interrupted Skipper as he was about to continue. 'What's this your name is, Professor?'

'Leonard McDonald Perrim. Whiskey angel.'

'I'll call you love, it's less complicated. I'll have some of that. I'm parched for something to give me a lift. Skipper you'll have to give me a jockey-back on the way back, I'm bunched. I've given you loads of jockey-backs in the past. Here, thanks love. You're a life saver. There's a great buzz from that.'

'Have some more, I've another bottle in my knapsack.'

'Thanks a million, love. I will.'

'Skipper, I think we've come far enough. What do you say we head down, after a rest?'

'I think your right, Albert. We've done enough for one day.'

Albert looked over at Eve. It was as though she had received a new lease of life as she gazed out at the scenery. The sky wore a metallic blue over Table Mountain, with a multicoloured rainbow that seemed closer than any rainbow they had ever seen before. To the right was the meandering Glenmalure Valley, and shooting from the back of the Sphinks rose a fire of still sun.

As they sat there agog with nature's beauty, it rained, but not on them. They could see a dividing line, not more than a hundred yards from where they sat, where the sweet rain swept into the

104

valley. They could see the purple haze of the mountains on the horizon.

Eve looked around and smiled. 'If I painted it Albert, no-one would believe me.'

The Professor stood up and took up his knapsack and a wooden box. 'I think it best we move. Should that rain move over here, we'll be all drenched.'

'Yes, he's right. Come on girls, let's make a start.'

They descended the incline through the gorse and heather, and the girls found new strength with the decline, aided by the fact that Albert and Davey linked Eve as Skipper and Donie linked Jill.

*

'Is there any chance of getting a bit of grub Mrs Fenton?'

'Were you on the hills then, Skipper?'

'We were, Mrs Fenton. The girls took to them like a duck to water.'

'How are you dear?'

'I meant to introduce you. This is Jill. Jill, you know Mrs Fenton.'

'George, would you ask the daughter could she cook up something for the party? Skipper, I'm glad to see you bring the wife away for the weekend. It's a bit of a holiday for her.'

'What are you talking about, Mrs Fenton? Didn't she have a week's holiday in the Rotunda Hospital last January, and I had to spend the whole week in the pub.'

'Don't mind him,' said Jill. 'You couldn't believe a word out of him. I'll have to have a drink.'

The Professor had moved beside them after arriving last to the bar. 'Allow me to get my friends a drink.'

Eve, Albert, Donie and Davey were taking off their heavy outdoor clothes.

'Ah, I'm not as fit as I used to be,' said the Professor.

'We weren't leaving you behind, Professor,' said Skipper. 'We had you within our sights. Do you mind me asking you, Professor, what's in the wooden box?'

'My autoharp.'

'I think I'll have a drink myself,' said Mrs Fenton as she poured the drinks. 'It could be a great night yet!'

'Sure that young girl there is the loveliest singer you ever heard. Not to mention the bold Skipper and Albert!' said the Professor. 'And what of my young friend there with the young lady?'

'God now, isn't that a strange one. I never heard Davey sing.'

'He can sing too, Mrs Fenton!'

'I never knew that.'

'That's his sister, Mrs Fenton,' said Skipper. 'That's telling you. I never knew myself.'

'There's very little you don't know, Skipper.'

The drinks were poured and yet another party had begun. The Professor produced his autoharp and played the finest collection of Carolan's airs that anyone of them had ever heard. Eve sang 'The Coolin', aided by the magical strings of the Professor.

The evening continued with a collection of ballads sung in perfect harmony by all concerned.

'We better make a move if were going back to the hostel,' said Skipper. 'The girls would be too tired to shack out in Stranahealy. They need a rest tonight. You're having a rest tonight, Jill, to charge your batteries for during the week.'

'I don't need sleep to charge them when you're around, Skipper. You charge them for me.'

'If we had a lift now you could all stay in my place,' said the professor.

'Come!' said Maurice. 'All cram into my Zephyr and I'll drive you over!'

Maurice had offered, and it seemed a good idea as everybody was having such a good time. They all climbed into the car like sardines and headed to Rathdangan.

*

The Professor's cottage was thatched, and the inside walls were woven in pine. To the Professors delight all agreed it was the nicest place they had seen.

'I'll have to make up some beds on the floor,' he said, 'but you're hardened men and I'm sure it won't bother you.'

Davey's eyes lit up as he looked over at the wall and saw a guitar. Unbeknownst to any except Eve, he had learned to play.

'Davey,' she said, 'if the Professor will let you, will you back me singing 'Tramps and Hawkers'? Because I think that's what we are. Do you mind Professor?'

'I certainly do not, and furthermore I would like to make him a present of it. It's an old Martin. You see I have an affiliation with him. I met him before, and although some of you thought me to be a homosexual, I'm not. He just reminds me of myself years ago. I would give all to have those years back with you young people. I'm sorry. I'm just a rambling old man.'

He was drunk and Skipper had detected a tear of sadness in the old man's grey eyes. 'You're always welcome in our company, Professor.'

'I'll retire to bed, so. Good night, my friends.'

'I think we'll all go to bed. Here put your sleeping bags down on the floor. You two girls can use that bedroom.'

'Come on in beside me Albert.'

'Come on stud. The night wouldn't be the same without you.'

Davey and Donie got into their sleeping bags, Davey with the guitar beside him. Albert got in beside Eve, and Jill beside Skipper as she extinguished the lights. There was a long pause. Skipper was snoring. Albert thought Eve asleep as he put his arms around her. It was an embrace made in heaven.

'I love you Albert.'

'I love you too, Eve. More than anything in the whole world.'

Fatigue was their sleeping pill.

20.

Peter Mulligan, Albert's neighbour, was sitting on the high stool.

'How are you, Peter? Are you here long?'

'Since Patrick's Day, my good friend.'

'Will you have a drink?'

'Hence the reason I'm in this establishment.'

'I've just come in to see Skipper and a couple of girls. Could I have a glass of Guinness, and what's yours?'

'A Paddy will be the order of the day.'

'That was a good winner the guard gave us.'

'We'd want to get them more often. Much to my detriment I was at the dogs last night, and our good friend Larry was there with a tip for a good thing. Trap five. Well the curse of the seven snotty orphans if I wasn't waiting on him for the jackpot.'

'He didn't win?'

'Win? The fucker couldn't catch the hare when he was stopped. He was a poor last if you know what I mean.'

In walked Larry and Terry.

'That's a bollix of a dog,' said Larry. 'I was talking to the owner, Peter. He said he never got the brake.'

'The brake? It's his neck should be broken. I was waiting for that fucker for the jackpot.'

'Here Einstein, are you buying a gargle? Young lad, what's this your name is, Albert? Did the toucher find his dog? Tell him not to be poxin' me over such trivialities.'

'Fair play to you Larry,' said Terry. 'You're able to use the big word.'

'Go and fuck off.' Larry had sat down beside Albert. 'Can I ask you a question? Here listen, a mate of mine is building a house. Can you get him the timber?'

'I could get him the trade price.'

'Trade price me bollix. Can you not rob it? I'll get Einstein here to pick it up in the bin lorry.'

The word 'rob' darted through Albert's spine. He had not spoken to anyone about his plans to steal money for Dale, and the coincidence of Larry mentioning his intentions was unpleasant.

'Ah, fuck it,' said Larry. 'You're too straight, I'll see Skipper.'

Albert kept his head down and listened as the conversation returned to dogs.

'I know fuck all about dogs,' Larry said. 'I hate them. One nearly bit the bollocks off me one day, and I running after a few fuckers.' Larry started laughing revealing his few bad remaining front teeth. 'I only started in the job. I was a bit heavier than I am at the moment. I must have been about twenty stone. I was heavier just before that, but I was after coming back from Tramore. Those fuckers sweated it out of me. Well it was my first day in the job, just where I am now, in Kevin's Street. It was about this time of year, and it was a nice day. But you know the way it is, one minute it's sunny and the next minute it's raining. Well I didn't know whether to wear a coat or not. Then this auld bollocks of a Sergeant sent me down to keep an eye on O'Connell Street, so I put on the coat so as not to be caught out. I wouldn't call it a coat, it was more like a knight in armour suit. I was sweating in the fucking thing, and to make matters worse didn't the sun start pissing down. As true as Jaysis, there was a smell from me. Well I was walking down Westmoreland Street, just coming to the bridge in O'Connell Street, and wasn't there this lorry stopped at the lights with four young lads scuttin' on the back. I wouldn't have

110

given a bollix only for this auld one gives me a look, and to add insult to injury doesn't the auld cow ask what have we got police for. Well I took to my heels and ran after the fuckers on the back of the truck, and as sure as oranges are pink didn't the lights turn from red to green. Come on you big fat bollocks, roared the young lads. Well there I was running down O'Connell Street and the truck about a hundred yards in front of me and going further with every trot. I was in a pool of sweat and I pissed in my trousers with the whole of O'Connell Street looking on. This Morris Minor drew up beside me. Give us a lift, says I to this auld one in the car. Get out of the way you fucking tick or I'll run over you, says she. Then I saw this big fucking dog running in my direction. Well, what does he do only grab hold of the fly of me pants. As true as God, I thought he was going to sever me middle leg. I didn't give a fuck who saw me – if I had a gun I would have shot the cunt in broad daylight. Ever since that day, I hate dogs.'

'Do you know the prostitutes up near Leeson Street?' said Albert.

'Of course I do, isn't me mot one!' said Larry. 'Don't bother about them. You can get a bird easy enough.'

'You know the fellas that look after them? What are they called? Pimps, isn't it?'

'Do you want me to look after a few birds for you?'

'No, I was just wondering are they ever caught, and what happens to them?'

'That's dangerous territory, son. Keep your voice down. You never know who would be listening.'

Eve, Jill and Skipper walked in, and Eve lit up with a smile as she saw Albert. He had seen her look beautiful before, but now... Albert's heart was startled with joy at her very presence.

'Hello lads,' said Skipper. 'Listen, do you mind if we move over here?'

'How are you, Albert?' said Eve. 'I'm on a high; I just sold one

111

of my paintings. I only met Jill and Skipper on my way in. Come on, we'll sit over here.'

'Come here, Skipper,' said Larry. 'I want to talk to you.'

Terry beckoned Albert over before they left the counter.

'Do you remember that question Larry asked me about Einstein? Do you remember he was trying to make a gobshite out of me?'

'Yes.'

'I got the answer from a mate of mine in the job.'

'You did?'

'Fucking sure I did. He worked out if you go to close to the sun you'll be burnt. I know we all know that now, but this was years ago before anybody knew anything. What do you think of that? Good, isn't it? I know they're only bin men, but there's some intelligent fuckers work in the Corpo! Well I don't mean work. You'd be sacked if you were caught working there. Listen Albert, I'll see you. You better join your mates. Jaysis! Your bird's a beauty, fair play to you.'

Skipper came over from the bar. 'I thought I'd never get away from that guard. Listen, the reason I asked you all here is because of the play. We'd want to get started. I've changed my mind about the play I want to do. There's too many in the cast of The Plough and the Stars, so I'm going to do Juno and the Peacock. Now Jill here is going to play Juno. Albert, you're playing Johnny, the son, and Eve you're playing Mary, my daughter. Now, we'll have to get Davey to play Jerry Devine. Now Donie, a mate of mine, he can't act, but he can play a furniture remover. Does anyone know anybody else?'

'What about the guard, Larry?'

'This is a serious play, not a pantomime,' said Skipper. 'We'll have to advertise in the press. The landlord in my place in Rutland Street is giving me a room upstairs so we can rehearse. So we're going to start next Friday at seven-thirty. How do you all feel

112

about that?'

Albert watched the excitement in Eve's eyes. He looked over at the other people in the pub. They all seemed to be looking at her mesmerising natural beauty. She laughed and talked with magnetic grandeur.

*

Eve and Albert were lying in bed, excited at the prospect of the play starting at last. They took turns reading different parts.

When they had finished, Eve turned to him. 'Hey Albert, tell me about yourself and your people.'

'Well, they come from a place called Galbally, outside Limerick. I lived down there until I was fifteen. Like yourself, there wasn't much work there, so my Dad got work in Dublin. That's how we came to live here. Although we hadn't much, it was a happy childhood. I suppose, like most things, my parents are best missed in their absence. But I still think of the beautiful mountainside. The Galtee Mountains and the magic flowing rivers. My folks are happy; but they weren't too happy to see me go live on my own. But we all must be alone sometimes to get on with our own lives.'

'You were an only child?'

'Yes, and I suppose a spoiled one. Will you tell me about your husband and child?'

Eve turned away and looked indifferent. 'Eugene McAllister's his name. He's a male nurse. Did you ever hear of a male nurse?'

'I never heard of such a person!'

'O yes, there is. Although I don't think he really was one. I think he was more of a doctor, or something. Two people. Dr Jekyll and Mr Hyde. He was a street angel, house devil. So the marriage lasted only two years.' Eve moved over towards Albert and cuddled into him. 'Only one good thing came from the

113

marriage, and there's only one thing I want to remember. My daughter, Jessica.' Tears welled up in her eyes and she collapsed against him.

'Don't talk about it now, Eve. Life has a way of sorting things out for the better.'

Albert got out of the bed and turned out the light. He took her into his arms, kissed her and lay in silence to let her savour her own thoughts. Occasionally he gave her a gentle squeeze to reassure her that she had found someone who truly loved her. In the ensuing silences they fell asleep.

21.

Eamonn was sitting at his office desk opposite Albert. He had the palms of his hands a distance apart facing one another in order to explain the size of a salmon bass he had caught.

Anthony passed him. 'Boasting again to the young lad about the enormity of your phallic symbol.'

'I'll give you the mountains Albert, but give me the sea. Ah, yes! Mornington. If you saw me there Albert, wrestling in the morning dawn with this bass. Just myself and himself. Him jostling with the waves and my hook about a hundred feet out in the deep. Me toying with the opposition.'

Albert was hardly listening. He looked intently at the clock cards he was turning in front of him. A cough came from Mr Broderick's office to remind the staff that he had arrived. Now he turned to the card with the fictitious name. Patrick Foley. He had the card neatly clocked, and as he thought of his misdemeanour his pulse began to race. He would have to take control of himself before approaching Mr Broderick's office to get them signed. His heart quickened again as he pondered the consequences of being caught.

He got up and went to the toilet room and looked in the mirror to see if his face looked in a natural state. Suddenly he realised the Patrick Foley clock card was newer than the rest. It did not have that used and worn look. The panic rose in him and he started to take deep breaths.

'Are you pumping the bike in there, Albert? Listen head, let's

115

in. I'm gumming for a smoke.'

Albert opened the door for Anthony – who looked startled to see him.

'Are you al right, Albert? You look like someone who's seen a ghost.'

'I did – Mr Broderick!'

'He's okay. Of course, you have to get him to sign the wages.' Anthony smiled. 'It'll be all right as long as you're not fiddling or anything.'

Albert stared in shock at Anthony through a cloud of smoke.

'I don't think you're yourself today, Albert.' Anthony lit his second cigarette from his first.

'I better go back,' Albert said, and he pushed his way out. 'Both of us are bound to be missed.'

When he got back and looked at the cards his suspicions were correct, for the new Patrick Foley card stood out like a goldfish in a pool of tadpoles. He eased the card to the floor and gently wiped it along the ground, using his shoe as a brush.

'Albert!' Mr Broderick shouted from his office.

It was as though someone had shot him in the back. He picked up the clock cards and headed towards his office.

'It's ten o'clock. I have to go out.'

'Sorry, Mr Broderick. They're ready.' He placed them with a shaking hand on the desk.

The shaking was nothing new in the company of Mr Broderick. Mr Broderick of course knew this, and capitalised on Albert's nervousness by constantly letting him know there were plenty of people available for work.

Mr Broderick looked at his watch and began signing them with speed. 'Did Eamonn check these? I haven't time to go over them in detail.'

'He did, Mr Broderick.'

The devil seemed to be on his side for he never saw Mr

Broderick sign anything so quickly.

Suddenly he stopped, and Albert's heart lurched.

'Patrick Foley,' he muttered as he scratched his head and looked into oblivion. 'Eamonn!' he shouted. He stood up, leaving the loose Patrick Foley card on his desk.

Albert was about to faint. He wondered if he could jump through the window for an early exit.

'Yes Mr Broderick?'

'Did Foley's finish that cargo into Bond Road yet?'

'Yes. They finished that yesterday,' Eamonn said. He looked down at the loose card on Mr Broderick's desk, wondering was there something wrong with the wages. Mr Broderick picked up the card. Albert was about to do a Superman through the glass window.

'Patrick Foley. Is he any relation to the Foley carriers?'

'No, Mr Broderick.' Albert spoke through a choking throat.

'Everything else alright, Eamonn?' He was signing the Patrick Foley card and moving on to the rest.

Albert's eyes were beginning to sting from the beads of perspiration dripping into his eyes.

At last, Mr Broderick was finished and was gone. Albert felt like someone reprieved from the electric chair.

'That's Scratchy gone for his coffee, Albert. Let's get ours.'

22

Skipper lived in the downstairs flat of a house on Rutland Street. Although he was generally thought to be married, it was untrue. He lived with his only sister, Trassie, who was wheel-chair bound. She adored her brother, and had been awarded huge compensation after her accident. As a result, she made sure Skipper was never in need.

It was above this flat that Skipper had procured a room for the rehearsals of Juno and the Paycock. He had placed an advertisement in the press seeking talent to fill the remainder of the parts in the play. Including the cast he already had, there was a motley crew gathered in the large room on the Friday. Skipper had brought Trassie up to observe the proceedings from her wheel-chair. She sat in the corner of the room.

Skipper addressed all, unfolding his intentions with an air of distinction: when he had the play ready for production, he wanted it to go on the All-Ireland festival circuit. It was the second time Albert had noticed a complete transformation in Skipper. The first had been when Skipper was apologising to Albert for invading his evening with Jill in the Pembroke lounge. Now, Skipper changed from his ordinary frivolous jesting self to an artist in control of his artistic endeavours. Albert watched as he started Jill and Eve in the opening act of the play. Every time Skipper stopped the play to give direction, Eve would look over at Albert and give him a pleasant smile.

Jill and Eve started impressively as Juno and her daughter

Mary. Skipper must have given Jill private lessons on acting, he thought. Albert was taken aback and excited at how good they were. He listened with bated breath for his cue.

It was during one of the pauses in the acting when they stopped for direction that Albert's eyes focused on the young man. He was sitting amongst the people who were awaiting an audition. He was tall and slim, his hair was blond and his eyes were a refined brown. Albert felt a jerk of jealously shoot through his body like a bolt of electricity as he noticed that the newcomer was smiling over at Eve. He had flawless looks.

'Would you read Jerry Devine, please?' Skipper asked the young man. 'What's this your name is?'

'Malcolm. Malcolm Knowles.'

The young man stood up and walked towards the acting area. Albert watched as he shook Eve's hand and smiled. Their eyes met, and Albert felt Eve would betray him as Jill had with Skipper before. Her face turned red as she looked over at Albert, putting her eyebrows at full height.

When the rehearsal was over, Skipper had cast the play. As he completed his finishing address, Eve rushed over to Albert and took his hand.

Malcolm walked over to join them. 'Is there anybody going for a drink? I'd like to join you.'

'Yes, come on,' Skipper said. 'We'll all go down to the Shakespeare.'

In casting the play, he had given the part of Jerry Devine to Malcolm.

*

Albert sidled over to Skipper in the pub. 'I thought you were going to give the part of Jerry Devine to Davey, Skipper?'

'He didn't want it. I asked him. I'm getting him to play the

119

IRA officer. It's a small part, but a better one. Jerry Devine is a thankless part. Here Albert, you'd want to go over to him. Look at him over there, chatting up your mot.'

Albert looked over and saw Eve talking to Malcolm. His heart heaved as he saw them smile. He immediately walked over and wedged his way between them, nudging Malcolm with his left elbow on his arrival.

'Malcolm has a lot of experience, Albert,' said Eve. 'He was with the Strand players. This is my boyfriend, Malcolm. His name's Albert Cagney.'

'I'm pleased to meet you. I admire your taste, she's very pretty.'

Eve bushed, bit her lip and tilted her face sideways.

Then all hell broke loose.

'You're some bollocks, Skipper! I saw that fucking ad in the paper, but that big thick red-neck of a culchie Sergeant wouldn't let me off. I'm a good actor! I'm acting all me life in the guards. Come here. Get's a pint, will you? Me mouth feels as dry as a camel's hole in a sandstorm. Have you a part for me? Barman, can I have another pint, please?'

Larry had burst in on the company, brushing the wet rain from his coat as he spoke.

'I think nearly all the parts are filled, Larry.'

'There's always room for a guard, Skipper. You never know when you might need them. I can get yous a couple of good uniforms.'

'I'll have to see how we're fixed Larry. I let you know.'

'Pass us over that pint Skipper, before it gets stale. Where do yous get the women from? Aren't they the two women we met in Albert's flat? I don't know how yous do it. You wouldn't want to see the yoke I'm married to. She's a face like a boxer dog. She's so big she had to get a prescription for a pair of knickers.'

'Your no oil painting yourself, Larry.'

120

'Ah, don't mind me in this uniform. You'd want to see me in my Sunday suit.'

'As long it's not your birthday suit.'

'Here, I'll see yous in a minute. I'm going over to annoy Albert and his queen bee.'

'See you, Larry.'

'Hey Albert, did you hear? The toucher found his dog. Actually it was Terry who found him pulling the bins apart. So you owe Einstein a pint, but here – you can get me one, I'll have it for him. Your name's Knowles, isn't it? I know your auld lad well. He has an electrical business.'

Albert looked over at Malcolm's unblemished features. He did not know him, but was already frightfully jealous of him: jealous of the fact that he had even spoken to Eve. She was holding Albert's hand tightly, as though she was being pulled away by Malcolm's charms. His thoughts froze and words began to fail him as he realized she could be taken away from him. He wondered if he should ask her to leave. But what if she said no, let's stay? Then he would know that she was attracted by his rival's handsome features. His nerves were getting the better of him as he stood there in silence.

'Here Malcolm?' said Larry. 'Slip us a score. I never got a chance to collect me wages. Your auld lad has plenty of poke.'

'Sure,' said Malcolm. 'Albert and Eve, what are you having to drink?'

'I think we better go Eve. I'm tired.'

There was a slight pause and Albert felt hot and cold, but then Eve stood up.

'Excuse me,' she said. 'I have to go to the ladies.'

'I'll just order one before you two leave' said Malcolm.

'Yes,' said Larry. 'Sit down, for fuck sake.'

'No,' said Eve. 'I'm tired too. Just give me a minute, Albert.'

Albert looked over at Malcolm with a mischievous smile on his face. He felt that he had won her – but for how long, he wondered. He took her hand and bid them all goodnight.

*

'I was so nervous going to the play,' Eve said. 'How do you think it worked? I think Skipper cast it well. He should have a good time doing it.'

'Yes. I hope so.'

They were lying on the bed. Albert had his two hands behind his head and was deep in thought. I think it's cast well, Eve had said. Did that mean she was glad Malcolm was playing beside her? Should he ask her about him? What she thought of him? If she knew he was jealous of Malcolm, she might use this fact in the event of any difficulties between them.

'Is there something the matter, Albert?'

'Do you really love me, Eve?'

She put her arm around him and pulled him towards her, smiling. 'Of course I do. You know that. Why ever should you ask? I've told you often, haven't I?'

'It's just I was jealous when I saw you looking at Malcolm. I thought you might run away on me with him.'

'You're the only one that matters to me, Albert. You need never be jealous.' She kissed him. 'But if you must know, there is something I don't like about you. I hope I don't insult you. It's your name, Albert. I think to me it sounds real English.'

Albert started to laugh and Eve joined in.

'I think you're right,' he said. 'You can call me something else if you prefer to.'

'Yes. I'll call you Ali. Ali's some sort of a king. You're my king. Will you come down to Carrow sometime with me, and meet my people?

'Yes, of course.'

122

'When Ali?'

'Why don't you ring in to my work tomorrow. Tell them you're my sister, and that I'm sick. Well go down to your folks, if that's not too short notice.'

'Would you mind if we called for Davey, and asked him to come down?'

'As long as we don't ask Malcolm.'

'Don't worry about him. Come on. We'll get up, call for Davey now and ask him to come.'

'At this hour of the night?'

'What the hell, let's have a midnight walk. You won't have to work tomorrow if we go to Carrow.'

23

They took the 7.30 a.m. bus. The Martin guitar was leaning against Davey as he lay slouched against the windowpane. On the opposite seat across the aisle, Albert sat looking out through the window with his arm around Eve. She was snuggled up beside him. Both Eve and Davey slept as the bus rustled through the countryside. He could smell the sweetness in the fresh air, and for a few instants he glimpsed a world of tranquillity. He looked over at Davey and then at Eve, and saw the resemblance that had eluded him before. He was astonished to learn that their different foster parents had not met before. Eve nudged him gently as she woke. She gave him a heart-warming, sleepy smile. Albert and his friends were away from the turmoil of turbulent city life. Dale and Mr Broderick were asleep in the back of his mind as he watched the yellow, brown, red and green leaves sail from the trees as the coach passed them.

After a long peaceful trip, they were in Westport. As they walked through the town, Albert observed people taking their life and work at a different pace. They had time to stop and talk and laugh, unlike those in the hustle and bustle of Dublin City.

'Let's go into a bar,' said Eve. 'I'll make a phone call to my Dad, ask him to pick us up. What do you lads want to drink?'

'A Guinness for myself and Albert, Eve. Is it far from here?'

'It's less than ten miles. I'll phone in a while.'

*

They walked down the road towards Carrowkennedy. Davey was silent and strangely apprehensive at the idea of meeting the people that had reared Eve. He walked alone, and to Albert he looked like a man deep in thought. Eve held Albert's hand, joyfully showing no concern.

James and his daughter Sinéad pulled up in the car and got out. Eve ran across the road with open arms, and was met with one of the warmest of embraces anyone could deliver.

Albert watched her stepfather. He had tanned skin, wore a friendly look and had a warm-hearted smile. Davey was pretending to look on, but Albert could see that he had his bashful eyes focused to the ground. Eve excitedly called them over, and after a welcoming introduction, Davey's bashfulness was put to rest. They entered the car and headed for Carrow.

Travelling for miles along the circuitous country road, they passed the mirror-surfaced Lough Moher. Albert watched with ecstasy as a family were reunited as the car motored through the desolate, barren, devastatingly-beautiful countryside. Eve and her family were saturated with talk of new and old news about people that neither Davey or Albert ever heard of. But they did not feel left out and enjoyed watching the bustling activity and talk from the others. Albert noticed Eve's sister as she smiled and talked, her face moving vivaciously.

They passed up a long driveway to a large two-storey farmhouse. Covered with ivy, it was the size of four of the houses Albert was used to seeing. Eve's mother was waiting at the doorway.

*

'Well, this is a special surprise, Eve dear.' Eileen, Eve's mother spoke as she served out dinner on a large, beautifully set table. 'We're very glad Davey came. We've been dying to meet him.'

'You'll have to come down and spend some time with us, Davey,' said James. 'You wouldn't think it, but sure there's plenty to do down here.'

Albert felt happy for him, for if ever anyone could, they were certainly making him one of the family. Albert watched as Eve's foster sister, Sinéad, looked over at his innocent face.

'And can he sing himself, Eve?' James asked.

Eve laughed. 'Not as good as me, Dad.'

'And what of Albert?'

Albert blushed. 'I heard Eve singing, Mr Robertson. That was enough to silence me.'

'He's being modest. Hey dad, will you bring us down to Killary Harbour? I want to make some sketches.'

'I will, surely. And how are you getting on with the paintings, Eve?'

'Good. I sold one only the other day.'

'Eileen, get yourself ready and we'll all go out for the day. Do you fish at all, Davey?'

'I try.'

'Sure we'll bring a couple of rods so, and maybe give an hour to it. That's an awful big looking box Davey has with him. It couldn't be a fiddle. It must be a cello if anything.'

'That's a guitar, Dad.'

*

Eileen remained at the house, but told them she would join them in the pub in Leenane later in the evening. They drove through a haven of soaring craggy peaks and forests of gnarled trees that shaded the country roads and shielded them from the sky. The meandering lanes through the silent lonely valleys filled

Albert's heart with peaceful solitude.

Perhaps he could get a job down here, he thought as they drove. Maybe James would give him a vacancy on the farm, and he could say goodbye to Dale and McEwan's. His heart quickened at the prospect of turning over a new leaf and getting back on the straight and narrow with the man above. After all, he had given him more that anyone could wish for; a girl he truly loved. He looked over towards her and found confirmation of their love in her eyes.

*

Eve and Albert climbed a small hill of rocks before sitting down and looking into the harbour. They could see James and Davey getting their rods ready for fishing. Sinéad was standing nearby looking out over the water.

'They're a lovely family, Eve.'

'Yes. I'm just looking at James helping Davey to prepare his rod. I could detect that look of sorrow in his eyes at the table. Did you notice how he always gave Davey the best attention when he spoke? I know it's his one ambition in life that never happened: to have a son of his own.' She looked at Albert with her alluring brown eyes and smiled.

'Would you like to have a son, Eve?'

'I would, Ali.' She looked away. 'I'm going to tell you something. What I told you about my child, Jessica. I'm a terrible liar. I told Davey the same. My husband had a child, Jessica. But she was from his first marriage.'

'You mean she wasn't yours? He was married twice?'

'Yes. I simply adored her, and I think she adored me. We went everywhere together, and she talked to me about everything. She even called me mum.' She spoke as though speaking to herself, as if Albert wasn't there. 'The sadness in my marriage was not

127

leaving him, but parting from her. When you think about someone as your daughter all the time, feelings build up in your mind until you actually believe them to be true. So it was with my Jessica.'

Sinéad's voice rang out on the breeze. She was talking and laughing with Davey like they had known each other for years. Davey had caught a fish, and there was much excitement between the three figures by the water.

'Yourself and myself will have a boy or a girl someday, whenever, Eve?' said Albert, smiling and putting his arms around her. There were tears in her eyes and her thoughts were laced with hurt. A chill of cold air swept to rage from the sea, across the craggy rocks where they sat. They got up and made their way to the harbour to join the family. Twilight was setting in and the evening drew nigh as the car moved off and headed to Leenane.

*

Word must have got around that something special in music was about to take place. Now, the small inn sold mainly beverages and groceries; on this particular evening there was little business doing in the grocery line. Beverages were being consumed and excitement was rising at the prospect of forthcoming music. Extra hands were brought to the fore to move the potatoes outside and to turn the entire premises into as spacious a bar as was possible. Empty orange boxes and beer cases provided the extra seating that was required.

The lively and colourful setting was filled with a healthy outburst of reels and jigs from James and Davey, with Sinéad on the tin whistle. Songs and poems were exchanged between the Robertsons and the other pub goers, with each song sounding better as the night wore on. Eve was swaying to and fro to the music, her arm around Albert. Their eyes were focused over towards Davey and Sinead, who seemed to hit it off like a perfectly matched couple.

'I don't think I've ever been so happy in my life, Albert. Look at Eileen and James, they're made for one another. I think there's something special in people who adopt children; seems they appreciate the goodness in nature more than most. Hey Albert, look at Davey and Sinead! They're kissing!'

Albert pulled Eve closer towards him and they smiled.

24

'Here, where are yous buying your drink? I wanted to walk home last night, not to run home. I'm sitting on that fucking pot all night. It's black scrambled eggs with piping hot gravy. My hole is in bits. Have you a part for me, Skipper?'

'I'm going to get you to read my part Larry and see how you get on. But once we start rehearsing, there's to be no messing or bad language.'

'Ask the butt end of my big bollix. Sure you're worse than myself!'

'Maybe so, Larry. But this is different. You see my sister is going to be in the room with us. And I'm the boss.'

'Jaysis! I never thought about it that way, Skipper.'

'I know, Larry. That's why I'm the director and can hire and fire anybody that acts the bollix. You're a guard, so be on your guard.'

'Here, give us a whiskey, barman. Would you do something about that toilet? There's no toilet roll in there. How are you Jill? What are you going to have? And you Skipper?'

'We'll have time for one or two. It's only five past seven.'

Albert and Eve were sitting down looking up at the counter at Skipper and Larry. The door of the bar opened and Albert's heart jolted when Malcolm entered. He was dressed impeccably and wore a charming smile. He first looked over at Eve and then darted a glance to Albert.

'Here! Knowles! Come here to me. You're going to be stuck

with a big hospital bill. They sold me bad drink with that score you gave me last week. And me stomach is in rag order ever since, not to mention the state of my hole. Give us another score and see if I can get better drink to rectify the matter.'

'Here,' said Skipper, 'mind what you're talking about in front of a lady.'

'I know what sort of a lady you are Jill. You're talking to Larry now. I'm no ordinary guard. I've been around.'

'Hey Larry! Are you trying to say my tart is a ride?'

Skipper and Jill laughed.

Malcolm bought some drinks and sat beside Albert and Eve. 'Have you read the whole play? I've read it about ten times, and each time I read it, it's better. Who's playing the part of Joxer?'

'I don't know.'

'God! You're looking really well Eve.' Malcolm said to Eve and then looked over to Albert.

There was a pause.

'Thanks, Malcolm.' Eve replied.

He smiled. 'And you too, Albert.'

*

Larry surprised everyone at rehearsals in Rutland Street when he read the captain. In point of fact he was just being himself. Together with a newcomer Skipper brought reading Joxer, it provided healthy entertainment and much encouragement for the rest of the cast. Albert watched Malcolm with Eve, and listened to his seductive voice. She must be attracted to him, he thought. He lacked the confidence in the part of Johnny he had had only a week before. He knew Skipper could see the weakness in him, but Skipper said nothing about it, and each time Malcolm and Eve sat down they were locked together in conversation. Albert felt completely abandoned, ignored. Something was happening, he

131

thought, and everybody knew about it except himself. When they stopped for tea, Eve stayed where she was to talk to Malcolm. Albert was alone as everybody else chatted in groups. So as not to make his hurt more noticeable, he went over to Skipper's sister and sat beside her.

'You look a little lost there.'

'You mean in the part, Trassie?'

'I mean in your eyes. You're too young to have problems. You've your whole life in front with worries without letting them start now. Look at me; bound to a wheelchair, but I have to accept it and get on with my life. I've learned to love life, and I do. I want to live forever. Did you ever hear the saying: laugh and the world laughs with you, cry and cry alone, the world has need for your laughter, for it has sorrows enough of its own. So is it a woman that's bothering you?'

'I'm not sure.'

Trassie smiled and put her hand on his shoulder, but he turned away with embarrassment. He saw Skipper looking at him and Eve gave him a welcome smile and a wave. Was he worrying over nothing? After all, they were together all the time; and now she was just talking to another member of the cast, however jealous he might be of Malcolm. Was he worrying in vain?

'I'm just rambling on,' said Trassie, 'interfering in something that's nothing to do with me.'

'No! Not at all.'

'I think I like to hear myself talking. But I would like you to know not to take life so seriously all the time. There are serious things in life that we have to take seriously. But in the midst of all we must find time for laughter. I mean, what's life without a laugh? And sometimes we may be depressed during the day, or when we wake up, but you'll find if you turn your mind away from your problems and think of something funny in the past you'll never go wrong. That's why I love Skipper so much. He makes me

132

laugh. Lose the cash in life, but never lose the dash.'

*

He held Eve's hand as they walked home. She spoke with excitement about the rehearsals, never mentioning Malcolm. Was he worrying unduly about him? Was Trassie right when she said that he was taking life too seriously? He loved Eve so much that he wondered if he should ask her to marry him.

When they got home and went to bed they made love, after which Albert lay back with his hands behind his head, deep in thought.

'Ali?'

'Hmm?'

'I'm moving into my own flat. My sister is coming up to stay for a while, and I told her she could stay with me.'

'Do you have to?'

`He held his breath. Perhaps Eve's heart had fallen prey to Malcolm's irresistible charms? Perhaps this was her way of telling him she had fallen for someone else? If this was so, he could not withstand the pain. He would never go with another girl. He would say nothing of his thoughts.

There was a long silence, and then she spoke. 'I love you, Ali. I love you more than anything in the world.'

'And I love you too, Eve.'

She put her arms around him and fell asleep. Before long a drowsy haze hit his own eyes.

25

An alarm went off in Albert's brain when Mr Broderick coughed.

In point of fact, to Albert it was more like a siren; for it was only nine o' clock and it was seldom if ever that Mr Broderick appeared before nine thirty. What was more significant and worrying was that it was Friday, and Albert had to somehow pick up the wages for the fictitious Patrick Foley.

Eamonn looked over and gave him a smile. 'Scratchy's wife must have fucked him out of bed early this morning. That's if she even sleeps with him – if her constitution is capable of absorbing such a heaving. He looks to me more like someone who has settled with choking the turkey. You don't look the best today. Had you a late one last night?'

'I'm fine, Eamonn.'

'At least the weekend is around the corner.'

Mr Broderick's door opened with a jerk and the office fell silent, like he had cast a magic spell over them. All conversations came to a halt along with Albert's heart.

'Any word on the strike, Eamonn?' said Mr Broderick.

'None as yet. '

'What time do you collect and give out the wages?'

'Well I collect them at twelve, sort them out and distribute them to the employees at four; save for a couple of wages Anthony requires for the lorry drivers who won't be back before the office closes. And the occasional one Albert may need for someone who's leaving early.'

Albert turned bright pink. Mr Broderick's eyes opened till the orbs seemed at the point where they were about to leave their sockets. He parted his legs and scratched his lower abdominal area with remarkable fury.

'Leaving early?' His voice echoed around the office, causing everyone to look around.

At this stage, Albert's head was on fire – so it was on him they all focused, causing the red hot charcoal skin on his face to glow even brighter.

'Who's leaving early, Albert?'

'No one, Mr Broderick Sir.'

He must have relieved the itch on the arch of his trousers, for his right hand now left his pocket and made its way to his head, combing the little hair he had with his fingers.

The eyes darted over to Anthony. 'How many drivers, Anthony?'

Anthony had his hand over his mouth in an effort to prevent Mr Broderick smelling the smoke from his breath; but his efforts were useless, the boss's eyes widened as he glared at Anthony's burnt fingers.

A small drop of oil fell on the door of Albert's heart. He felt it ease open and begin to move again with a faint squeaky beat as the attention was momentarily lifted from him.

'Two drivers are going to Galway, Mr Broderick,' said Anthony. 'They won't be back 'til the small hours.'

'Give those two wages only, Eamonn. Nobody else. Did Foley's Carriers bring up timber today, Eamonn?'

'The first load was up here at nine this morning.'

Mr Broderick put his hand to his mouth and coughed his way out of the office.

Albert had a strange feeling that Mr Broderick knew more about Albert's exploits with the fictitious Patrick Foley than he pretended. After all, he had brought the wages strangely into question and then sternly refused to give other wages out to anyone except the late drivers. How was he going to collect the packet? Was Mr Broderick just waiting for him to make an effort so he could nip the plan in the bud?

Albert got to his feet, walked over to Anthony and whispered to him. 'Anthony, could I see you in the cellar?'

'Listen head. We can't both leave at the same time. Scratchy is still inside scratching his balls, standing by the radiator. You go and I'll follow you in a minute.'

*

The cellar was just beside the toilet, with an entrance six feet by three with an open-plan wooden stairs to the bottom floor. It was a large dark room with stacks of mouldings and old used stationary from yesteryear which gave a strong musty odour. Frightened, Albert waited at the corner. All that could be seen was a square light with the shadow of the stair trusses of the stairway.

Then there was a large silhouette of a man walking down the steps, the sound of his feet echoing as they hit the wood. A blaze of light from a match lit the room like a lantern for a few seconds.

Anthony exhaled and a puff of smoke exploded into the musty air. 'For fuck's sake, head. Have you no respect for my lungs, bringing me down to inhale this mouldy air?'

'I'm in real big trouble, Anthony.'

'Did Scratchy catch you smoking?'

'Much bigger troubles than that; but I can't tell you about it now, it would take too long. But I'll tell you this evening. I need to ask you a great favour.'

'What's that, Albert?'

'I need you to collect the wages for a young lad, Patrick Foley, but not to tell anyone I asked you.'

136

'Listen head, you heard Mr Broderick. Anyway, why can't you ask Eamonn yourself? I mean he's a mate of yours.'

'I can't. Just do it for me, please?'

There was a sudden tremendous clattering roar from above and it seemed as though the roof was about to cave in. Albert grabbed Anthony's arm.

'For fucks sake, head! What's that? You haven't sent the wrath of God upon us!'

There was a hammering of hooves, the frantic bellowing of a farmer, and then the thunderous clout of a cow thumping down into the cellar.

When Albert and Anthony had returned to their senses, the cow was up after its fall and was walking towards them. Albert stood pinned to the wall, and Anthony was choking, having swallowed the lighted cigarette. The cow stood still and gave a concussed moo, which caused a crowd to appear at the stairway. Mr Broderick left his office and walked through the spectators.

'What's all the commotion, Eamonn?'

'A farmer with a herd of cows was passing. Some off them strayed into the yard. One of them fell into the cellar, and he went away without missing him.'

'He's down there?' said Mr Broderick, pointing at the entrance from a distance. 'What on earth can we do?'

'I was in a position like that before, years ago,' said Skipper. 'An auld cow had me caught in a hole. She wanted me to marry her.'

'We could shoot her in the hole, cut her up and bring her up as beef,' Eamonn suggested. 'It's near enough to Christmas. Beef! What else can you get from a cow?'

'You can get a doze of the clappers,' said Skipper. 'I did, from an auld cow in Ringsend.'

Mr Broderick did not smile. 'Ring the guards in Kevin Street Eamonn! Immediately!'

137

In the cellar, there was nothing but silence from above; the crowd seemed to have dispersed. When the cow turned away to the other side of the room, Anthony and Albert made a dash for the stair exit. Anthony got out first, but as Albert emerged Mr Broderick was just leaving his office and locked eyes on him. Albert stood panting.

'What on earth were you doing down in the cellar?'

'I was trying to push the cow up the stairs, Mr Broderick.'

'Leave that to the guards, Albert. They're getting paid for the likes of that. You've surprised me, brave young lad you are. I would never have the courage to do such a thing. I'm going down to George's Street. Tell the staff I'll see them later.'

Minutes later, Larry parked his bike outside the timber office and entered, puffing and blowing and gasping for breath.

'Is there someone trying to set me up? Someone rang the station and said my mot was caught in some cellar, and she couldn't get out?'

'There's a cow caught in the cellar over there!'

'Yeah, that's her. Are you the smart bollocks? Are you Mr Coyle or Mr Broderick?'

'No, neither. Mr Broderick's not here. I'll get you Mr Coyle.'

Uncharacteristically, Larry Coyne extended his hand as Eamonn came to the counter. He had a smile on his face, and tried to speak in a voice that was courteous and foreign to his nature. 'Mr Coyle Sir, I've been sent down about a small problem you have in the cellar. I'm a good friend of Albert Cagney and Skipper – I mean Christy McCabe.'

'A farmer was passing with a herd of cows, they strayed in the yard and one fell into the cellar' said Eamonn.

Larry smiled. 'Would this be a human cow, perhaps strayed from a women lib march about burning the bra, or a jersey cow? Would anybody have a rope?'

A crowd of workers gathered at the top of the stairway as the guard went down with the rope. Boisterous moos could be heard from below.

*

When Albert went to look for Anthony, he found he had already gone to Kenny's. He walked up Golden Lane towards the pub trying to hold his composure and think how he was going to explain about Dale's threats and Patrick Foley's wages.

As he opened the side door, the sound of talk in the crowded ale house and the stale smell of smoke and beer hit him. He panned his eyes around the pub, and saw in the far corner a cloud of smoke containing the form of Anthony.

He made his way over. 'How are you, Anthony? Would you not try and give up cigarettes? I believe they shorten your life and cause cancer.'

'Listen head, I'm having a few pints and I don't need lecturing. What do you mean shorten your life and cause cancer? In thirty years time they will have a cure for cancer. It will only be a tablet. I mean head, thirty years ago they used to say as mad as the man on the moon, now people are booking holidays for a trip up there. Are you having a pint? What happened about the cow? Did the guards come? I slipped off early because I knew Scratchy wouldn't be back.'

'They sent a guard on a pushbike, Larry. I met him before. Do you know him?'

'No.'

'He got the cow out.'

'Did you give your lad his wages?' Anthony looked at Albert with a sparkle in his eye as he watched the blood run to his face. 'Don't fuckin' tell me there is no such person as Patrick Foley and you made up the wages to rob them?' Anthony laughed, then stopped to draw on his cigarette like a stricken asthmatic would on

139

oxygen.

Albert took the pint to his mouth and took as big a gulp as was possible. 'That's it. I had to do it. That's what happened.'

Anthony momentarily froze solid and took such a pull from the cigarette that the ash at the top was half an inch long. He looked around the pub in stunned silence. 'Listen, head, are you fucking serious? You'll get both of us sacked. You're after getting me involved because I collected that wage. You better sort this out head – because this is big trouble!'

The door opened and in walked Skipper and Larry. The perspiration was dripping from the guard.

'I'm no fucking idiot,' Larry said. 'Myself and Skipper brought that cow up to that farmer, and the decent auld lad gave us a tenner.'

'You told him you'd do him for having no tax on his car if he didn't.'

'I was only messing.'

'He got the message.'

'That Mr Broderick is a nice auld lad. Would he give me a job if I left the guards?'

'D-did he come back?' Anthony interrupted.

'Yeah,' Skipper said, 'and he was looking for you.'

Anthony's pale frightened face looked over at Albert. 'Listen head, we're bollixed and I think I'm about to puke.'

'I'm sorry, Anthony.'

The far door of the pub opened, and there standing in the frame was Mr Broderick. Now it was rare that Mr Broderick would walk into a workman's pub, though he had once called into this very pub on discovering one of the company's lorries parked outside. Albert sat still with shock and Anthony was frozen speechless. From the sudden smell in the air, it was apparent that Anthony's bowels had evacuated without warning.

Mr Broderick tightened his face, giving everyone who saw him a fright and none more so than the culprits. He pointed his index finger at Anthony and rolled it around in a u-shape towards himself. Anthony fell off the stool, and only managed to get up with help from Albert. He walked unevenly towards the door, as though he was about to mount a wild horse. There was foam dribbling from his mouth.

'Are you buying a round, Mr Broderick? I'm the one that got that cow out for you.'

Mr Broderick pushed out into the street, with Anthony following in an uncomfortable trot.

'Typical mean bollix. That's the last cow I'll get out of a hole for him.'

'How are you getting on learning the lines, Larry?'

'I'm under pressure in the job. Give us a bit of time.'

'I'm not going to mess around with this play. I'll expect them off in the next two weeks. Were you ever on the stage before?'

'Amn't I on the stage all me life, for fuck sake. You have to be to survive in the guards.'

Albert's eyes lit up with anxiety as Anthony returned.

'He's some cheek calling in here after working hours,' said Larry. 'Did he slip you anything for my services? What did he want? Did he say anything about me? A job well done?'

'He never mentioned you.'

It was only when Skipper and Larry started talking together that Anthony could explain. Mr Broderick had only looked for him because he saw one of the lorries parked in town and was inquiring as to where the lorry should have been.

Albert felt at ease once more. It was not the first time his blood had raced, lately. Why, with Jill and Dale his heart had become accustomed to sudden gear changes. Now the Patrick Foley episode was shared, halved with Anthony, his unwilling confession box. Anthony had taken half the evil weight from his shoulders just by knowing about the misdemeanour.

'Listen head, this is not the end of this. You got me involved, and you're going to get me out of it as quick as you got me in even if I have to go and tell the truth.'

'I'm really sorry, Anthony. I had no choice, but I promise I'll make it up to you.'

'I don't want fuck all of that, head.'

'It's not for me. Come on home and I'll explain it to you. The whole gang are going to the Neptune tonight. Come with us and I'll work it out.'

*

When Albert walked up Leeson Street, he noticed someone sitting on the steps of his flat.

'Do you know what I'm going to tell you, mate? I knew from the minute I saw you, you were sound. How did you enjoy your pint in Kenny's, and of course the Glen of Imaal that weekend you were there? I see you brought Jill along with you. I tell you one thing pal, Dale misses fuck all. Now, down to business. Have you my shillings?' Dale smiled, and Albert could see two gold fillings in his front teeth.

'I have to go upstairs, I won't be long.'

'Hurry up. Like I said, I knew I would have no problem with you.'

Albert eagerly made his way up the stairs and sorted out the money for Dale. He had seen too much panic already in the evening with Mr Broderick and Anthony for even Dale to cause him more concern; especially since he had the finances to meet Dale's demands.

'Let's make it this time every week, Albert.'

'Okay.'

Dale climbed into a waiting car. Albert stood collecting his thoughts on the pathway when he heard his name called. He looked around. Malcolm walked towards him.

'Hello, Albert. I was just around the area and thought you might be in. I was wondering were you doing anything tonight? Would you like to go for a few drinks, or whatever?

He was dressed immaculately, his hands on the pockets of his Crombie overcoat, and he looked reticently away from Albert as he spoke. Eve had left his flat this very day because her sister was coming to Dublin, and now Malcolm was at his doorstep. Albert had not realised that Malcolm knew where he lived. Eve must have told him; and now he had come to tell him that he had become Eve's lover. His stomach heaved as he imagined Malcolm with Eve.

'How did you know where I lived?'

'Eve told me the other night.'

'Yeah?'

'I hope you don't mind me calling.'

They went up to the flat in silence. He would let him speak; let him confess and explain. Whenever in a tight situation, Albert always put his foot in it. Eve had said nothing to him about them, nor had he asked her about him, except that first night Malcolm and herself had met. Eve had reassured him that he was the only one.

Yet what of the long conversation they had had together on the night of the rehearsal?

'You seem a little taken back by my intrusion,' said Malcolm. 'It's just I'm so excited about the play, and I enjoy the company of all the players. I suppose I'm what you would call a loner. I, ah, don't have a lot of friends that I pal around with. In point of fact I don't have any. You have a lovely girlfriend, Eve. I was talking to her the other night. You're lucky, she's really nice. I envy you.' He had his head down as he spoke, and was nervously twitching his fingers.

Albert was more than confused. Surely he could have all the

143

friends he wanted? He had not said much about Eve. Once again, had he put the cart before the horse?

'What were yourself and Eve talking about?'

'The play. And another play I was in, Villa for Sale.'

The doorbell rang. When Albert answered it, he was greeted by Eve, Sinéad and Davey. Everyone seemed so happy that Albert wondered was he putting himself into turmoil over nothing.

'Malcolm is upstairs!'

Eve came over to Albert and gave him a warm embrace. He had watched her face as he mentioned Malcolm, but she had shown no sign of indifference. Davey and Sinéad were holding hands.

'I've got something very important to tell you,' said Eve, smiling. 'About us. When we're alone, I'll tell you about it.'

*

Jill, Skipper, Eamonn and Anthony joined the others at the Neptune Rowing club, so Malcolm did not feel out of place. Eamonn introduced himself and the others to the assembly.

Anthony gave Albert a formidable look though a fog of smoke. During the hours of their separation, he had obviously made a long mental inspection of Albert's thievery and decided that if he got Albert on his own he would happily choke him.

'Eamonn?' said Skipper. 'Can you act? I'm getting a bit worried about Larry learning these lines. He's hitting the gargle a bit heavy.'

'I'm afraid not. Why not try Mr Broderick?'

Malcolm was sitting at one side of Albert, Eve on the other. Albert felt wedged between them. He had purposely sat down first. Eve sat beside him, and though he expected Malcolm to sit beside her, he did not.

They drank and laughed and talked all night like old friends.

Davey, Albert, Skipper and Eve got up to sing. When the pub hours came to a conclusion, they walked home in spritely form, singing to their hearts content.

'Albert? Is it alright if I stay with you tonight? I want to give Sinéad and Davey a little time to get to know each other. I also want to ask you something regarding a bit of news I've got.'

Eve leaned over and kissed Albert just after she had spoken, and Malcolm turned away.

'Of course you can. You know you don't have to ask me.'

*

Eve sat on the bed beside Albert. He was sure now as he held her hand that he had not lost her to Malcolm. Her eyes were childlike and truthful. Why didn't he try and live life without worrying all the time? If he loved Eve and she him, then surely he must trust her. A pink tinge warmed his face as he thought of how possessive he was of her. She was looking at him with those brown, stunning eyes, and she must have read the thoughts in his mind for she gave a reassuring smile.

'My father sent me up this pile of money with Sinéad. He didn't give it to me when I was down there. He knew I wouldn't have taken it. I really love you Albert, and I want the two of us to go away together for a few months, anywhere. Just let's take a house somewhere. Somewhere I can just paint and be with you.'

'That's sounds lovely. But what about my job?'

'Why, you told me with the builders strike they'll be doing hardly anything. Anyway, we wouldn't be going straight away. We have the play to do first.' She smiled and pulled him close. 'Let's make love and fall asleep thinking about it.'

And this they did.

26.

The autumn leaves withered and vanished into oblivion, and indeed by winter the play had still not got off the ground. There was considerable concern about the guard, Larry. Firstly Skipper wondered whether he would ever learn the lines of the Captain. Also, as the weeks of autumn and winter passed he came less and less to rehearsals, and when he did attend he was the worse for drink. However, for the others the rehearsals turned out to be a great exercise in companionship and friendship. An unbreakable bond of love was cemented between Albert and Eve during those months. Albert did not see much of Davey, for Davey now spent almost all of his leisure time with Sinéad. By contrast, Malcolm became his constant companion, and called in to the flat almost every evening after work. It no longer worried or bothered Albert when Malcolm came out with himself and Eve.

It was nearing the summer when Eve and Albert began their plan to move to a small cottage in the Glen of Imaal that Eve had rented. Albert had found the courage to tell Eve about Dale. She would give Albert the money to pay Dale for the weeks they were away, during which time they would ponder upon same. Together they would have to come up with a more permanent solution.

*

'Here! Buy us a gargle and don't make a fucking show of me. I'm on the floor. Skipper will have to put a halter on the play. I

146

have to go into John of God's for a couple of weeks!

'He was looking for you.'

'I know, I know, I fucking know. Don't pox me now when I'm drinking. Enough listening to her this morning without you starting at me.'

Larry Coyne was sitting at the counter with Peter Mulligan, Albert's neighbour, in Mc Daid's public house as Albert entered.

'How do you learn those fucking lines?' Larry said. 'Do you have to have one of those picture memories or something? I have the gist of them. It's just that they're coming out arseways. I remember getting the hand torn off me years ago in school for not learning that, 'I wandered lonely as a cloud'.'

'Not too lonely, I detect,' said Peter. 'You're still able to enjoy a few pints?'

'Can you remember where you were when President Kennedy was shot?'

'I can't remember where I was yesterday, my good man. You'll get the hang of them, I dare say, whenever. Sure there's no hurry with the play. I suggest we beef into plenty more porter; they'll come to you sooner or later. I imagine possibly later. But sure we never died a winter yet.'

'Is this the first play you've done, Larry?' Albert asked.

'It's the fucking last, I tell you. I was in a pantomime years ago. Where you ever in a show when at the end nobody claps the cast, and as soon as the prompter walks out, he gets a standing ovation?'

The door of the bar opened.

'Here Knowles? I owe you fuck-all. I gave you back that score, a couple of months ago, when I got me job savings. Here, I'll have to borrow it again.'

Malcolm had just come in looking for Albert. He bought a round of drinks, and asked Albert would he sit down and join him in a snug at the corner of the pub. His voice seemed disjointed;

Albert noticed a worried look on his face.

'Are you going to the glen, the weekend?' said Malcolm.

'Yes. We're all going.'

'Is Eve going?'

'No. She's going down to Carrowkennedy with Davey and Sinéad to stay with her folks. Why do you ask?'

Malcolm's face twitched nervously and he turned away from Albert. 'Would it be okay if I come? I want to get a chance to talk to you alone.'

'Sure, you can come. But can't you talk to me here? Is there something the matter?'

'I can't explain it. I just can't. Will you sit with me alone, in the Glen, and I'll try explain? Just for a while.'

Albert looked up. Malcolm was crying. He stared frightfully into Albert's face for a moment, then pulled his eyes away and hurriedly made an exit from the pub without saying another word. Albert stood up and looked on in bewilderment.

'What the fucks the matter with him?' said Larry. 'He nearly knocked me down off the stool passing me by, and never passed a comment or said goodbye. Did yous have a row or something?' He looked in surprise at his empty glass. 'Here Albert, get us a brandy. I'm not getting paid until tomorrow.'

'I didn't have a row with Malcolm. He's only after giving you twenty pounds. That's three weeks' wages to me.'

'Don't be moaning, for fuck sake. Here, I'll buy you a gargle. Are you having one Peter?'

'Hence the reason I'm in this establishment. I'll join you with a large brandy.'

'I have to go,' said Albert.

'Sit down, for fuck's sake. It's like a brothel here, with men running in and out every five minutes.'

27

'Top of the morning, Albert. I'll have to hand it to you as the blind man said to the prostitute. She's a gorgeous looking girl, and an added bonus in the fact that she's a lovely singer. There's Scratchy after making his entrance. I was hoping someone would ring in and say he wasn't coming.'

Albert sat opposite Eamonn as he spoke. Mr Broderick's office door opened and he marched up the office floor deliberately coughing until he came to a standstill in front of Eamonn. He balanced on one foot like a trapeze artist on a tight rope and scratched himself.

'Yes, they're never happy. The builders strike was supposedly fixed up months ago, now there's talk of it starting up again. They're never happy. I don't think they deserve work at all.'

'I heard they definitely will go on strike this time.'

'Are those wages ready, Albert?'

'They are, Mr Broderick.'

'I have to go to George's Street. I'll sign them later.'

When Mr Broderick left, Albert got up and walked over to Anthony.

'Will you come over yonder, I want to see you to tell you something.'

'Listen head, I'm not going down that cellar to witness flying cows. I'm dying for a smoke though. I'll see you in the jacks.'

*

Albert was hit by a wall of smoke as he opened the toilet door. Anthony was sitting in the dense fog.

'Sorry Anthony, I didn't know you were using the toilet.'

'You're alright head, I'm not. At least I hope I'm not, because I never lifted the lid.'

'I wanted to see you about Patrick Foley's wages.'

'Listen head, I've feel I've aged about ten years since this episode. I get the feeling people are looking at me with suspicion. I'm smoking heavier than I ever did and I'm drinking as though it's going out of fashion.'

'What I wanted to tell you was I stopped doing wages for him. I'll sort out my problem another way. I'm going to tell Mr Broderick Patrick Foley left. I bought you a lighter. It's a Ronseal, just to thank you and tell you I'll be paying the money back.'

'It's just as well head, because we're all going out on strike shortly.'

'Are you coming to the Glen at the weekend?'

'Okay, but I'm not walking up those mountains.'

28.

'Donie met his young lad the other day as he was coming home from the pub. Daddy, says he, your dinner is burnt. How can it be burnt and we're having salad? It's in the back of the fire! What do you think of that, Mrs Fenton? Nancy's a women libber merchant. You know, burn the bra – although she doesn't need one.'

'Go along and fuck off Skipper,' said Donie. 'I'm the boss in my kip. When I got married, I took the trousers off and handed them to Nancy. See those, says I. You mend them and I'll wear them.'

'Donie, the only way you get out is to say to Nancy, give us that washing love and I'll hang it on the line! And then you hop out over the wall.'

They were sitting in the bar in the Glen of Imaal.

'What about your mot Jill, Skipper? I'm not saying anything against you Jill, but he's bringing you away every weekend. You have a hold on him?'

'The only hold I have on him, Donie, is the hold he wants.' Jill lifted the corner of her skirt, revealing her suspenders. 'He likes his queen bee.'

'Are you not one of those women libbers, Jill?'

'I wouldn't be a part of that holy-knickers crowd. They think their knickers is a tabernacle. You have to pray to get into them, and should you do the slightest thing wrong they'll excommunicate you.'

Mrs Fenton was cleaning the counter, smiling at the assembly.

'God though Professor, you couldn't be up to these young people nowadays. We weren't like that in our day?'

'More's the pity, my good lady. Sure let them enjoy themselves. Why not decorate the counter, on me?'

The door opened and when Albert looked around he saw Malcolm. He was unshaven and looked drunk. He looked over at Albert, but then turned away and escorted himself to the opposite end of the bar.

'What's the matter with him, Albert?' Skipper asked.

'I don't know. '

'Did you hear about Larry?'

'I know. He can't learn the lines.'

'Not only that. He was taken in to John of God's for a drying out programme. I wonder; is it because the play is over that Malcolm is in bad form? I know he was looking forward to it. He was very good playing Jerry Devine. I mean, it's a thankless fucking part. He's a nice sort of a fella. I don't like to see him let down. I'll go and have a word with him.'

'Stay where you are, Skipper. He said he wanted to see me on my own.'

Albert got up from the chair and walked off towards the other end of the bar. Malcolm had asked to see Albert alone, but he had forgotten until now. As he approached, Malcolm looked at him with melancholy eyes.

'Are you all right, Malcolm? I was expecting you to call me if you were coming away.'

'You were going with them, so I got my father to leave me to Donard.'

'You're drinking whiskey. It's not for me to say, but don't think that's a little heavy? It's only after seven. Is something major the problem?'

'What do you want to drink?'

'I've got two drinks down there with the lads. Don't you want to come down to join us? There's only Skipper, his friend Donie, Jill, Anthony and the Professor. You don't know the Professor, but you'll find he's a fine old man.'

'I have to see you alone. I want you to come into the lounge; I've got something to say to you.'

'Okay Malcolm. I'll just get my drinks. If you don't want to come down, do you want to wait in the lounge and I'll join you in a couple of minutes? I just have to excuse myself from the lads for a while.'

Albert made his way back.

'What the fuck's going on down there? Is it a private party? Are you going to do the play on your own?'

'No Skipper. I'm just talking to Malcolm on his own about something personal. I'll only be a while.'

'Well hurry back, yourself and Malcolm. There will be a sing, dance or show your mickey party starting shortly.'

Albert picked up the drinks and walked towards the other lounge. Malcolm was sitting in the far corner, as far away from anyone as was possible. When Albert sat down he could see he was trembling. He certainly had a lot of drink on him. He is going to tell me he's an alcoholic, Albert thought as he sat down.

'I don't know how to tell you what I have to tell you. I've been trying to think how to put it all week.'

'What do you mean, Malcolm? What's this all about? Is it drink?'

'I'd feel better if it was. I can't eat, I can't sleep, I can't think. And if I do sleep it's only in nightmares. Nightmares that keep reminding me that a horrible future for me is near at any moment. Devils and serpents watching over me at night, reminding me of my sorrow. Leaving me on the bed unable to move, unable to speak, unable to call for help. Watching over me with agonizing torture, until dawn, till they let me walk again and face my dilemma.'

153

'Do you mean you've been in the horrors from drink? Seeing rats and that, running up walls? Like in the film, The Lost Weekend.'

'No. Much worse than that!'

'Do you know what causing all this, then?'

'Yes, you.'

'Me, Malcolm? What did I do?'

'I never thought there was such a thing, but I'm madly in love and I just don't know what to do.'

Albert stood up with stark bewilderment. His pulse began to race, and he felt threatened.

'I glad you came to tell me, Malcolm. But I'm afraid I can do nothing for you. Eve's my girlfriend. I'm in love with her, and there's no way you can have her.'

'I don't want her, Albert. I'm not in love with her.'

'Who is it then you're in love with?'

'You, Albert.'

Albert sat down and picked up his pint, taking a big gulp. 'Me? Maybe I'm drunk, Malcolm, but I'm on a different wavelength. I don't follow you.'

'You. Yes, you. I don't know how it came about, but you never leave my head. Every time I see somebody near you, talking to you, I cringe with jealousy. I can't bear to see someone touching you, save for myself.'

The blood rushed to Albert's face, and he felt more than uncomfortable. He was getting flashbacks now of all the times Malcolm had called to him of late, even at work; the way Malcolm had looked at him over the past weeks, the way he had smiled at him for little reason. There was a long silence.

'I don't know what to say, Malcolm. I think you should find yourself a girlfriend. I mean, you're a good-looking guy. You'd have no problem there.'

'Will you be my best friend, Albert? I'll do anything for you. I give you anything money can buy.'

Albert looked at his pleading face, and forced a smile. 'Let's go out to the lads.'

'Yes, Albert. I'm sorry, but thanks.'

Albert and Malcolm sat down beside Skipper and his friends in the bar.

'You have a forlorn look on your face sitting there, Albert. I think you're sorry already you didn't bring Eve. As you can see, I brought Jill.'

'And I'm on the pill, Skipper.' Jill laughed.

'Donie wouldn't bring Nancy. He left her at home, where she'll be chancy.'

'Fuck off, Skipper. My mot does everything for me because she loves me.'

'She loves me, yeah, yeah, yeah!'

'What's the three most important qualities a man sees in a women Professor?' Jill asked.

The Professor smiled. 'Good lips, good hips and nice fingertips.'

'No it's not,' Skipper interrupted. 'That she doesn't tell, she doesn't yell, she doesn't smell, and doesn't swell.'

*

They walked into the mild summer night. The night sky was dark yet inviting, for the moon changed the darkness to twilight. Skipper and Jill walked ahead, swinging linked hands to the lilt of the song they were singing. Donie and Anthony were behind.

Even further back were Malcolm and Albert. A cold shiver bolted through Albert's body when Malcolm reached out his hand to take hold of Albert's. There was a sense of panic in his mind, and he looked ahead for inspiration. He could see the back of Donie and Anthony. Great puffs of smoke rose in front of

Anthony's head and were swallowed immediately by the fresh midnight air. If only somebody would turn around and say something to embarrass Malcolm. Albert felt he needed Skipper to do his talking.

A distorted moonlit sky was reflected on the Slaney River as they crossed the bridge, and the trout darted to and fro at the oncoming intrusion. It chilled a little towards dusk, and you could smell the newly moved hay from the meadow.

29.

They were in the hut behind the panel planer. Skipper was reading the paper, and two of the other workers were just standing there smoking as Albert approached them.

'So the builders are gone on strike at last. Today is their first day. They'll have us out in a week.'

'Skipper? Could you come into the plywood shed and move a couple of sheets for me?'

Albert was excited to speak to him alone. 'You won't believe this.'

'What?'

'You know Malcolm. I don't know how I'm going to tell you this. Do you remember he was on his own in the Seskin Pub and he called me aside?'

'Yeah. What of it?'

'You won't believe this. He told me he loved me. I mean, Jesus, I'm serious. He was serious. I got a fright. What am I suppose to say to him. Will you talk to him?'

Skipper closed his eyes bursting in laughter. 'You mean he's a fairy, a bum-boy, a pigs-ear, a queer?'

'I don't know. That's more or less all he said.'

'What does he want you to be, the man or the woman? To give or to take? I'm not getting on too well with Jill. Do you want to buy the suspenders and garters I bought for her from me? I'll give them to you at half price? I'd say they'll fit you. I'll bring them in tomorrow, you can try them on.'

'Fuck off, Skipper.'

'Anyway, Jill and myself are gone past that stage. Are you going to start wearing make-up and that sort of thing? You'll have to practise your walk. Wait till Mr Broderick sees you. Maybe he'd bleedin' fancy you.'

'You can fuck off, Skipper. I'm no queer.'

Albert stormed out of the plywood shed and left Skipper standing there laughing to himself.

*

'In case you don't believe me, I brought you in a photo of myself and the fish. It weighed 7 pounds, 12 ounces. In point of fact; if that was a competition in the Knights of the Silver Hook Club, it would have taken first prize. Now I'm six-foot three. So what size would you say he is?'

'God, Eamonn. He's a big fish. And you caught him in Mornington? I'd say he must be 15 inches.'

The door opened and Mr Broderick emerged, combing his hair with his hand and then brushing the dandruff off his lapels.

'Well Eamonn? It's not looking good. They went out on strike this morning. We'll have to prepare to let the men go.'

'Hmm. I suppose there's no chance it will only last a day or two?'

'We must be prepared for the unexpected.'

He lifted his leg high like a ballet dancer and negotiated an enormous scratch between his arch. His upper lip tightened and his nose cringed; then he stood as though relieved.

'I'm going down to George's Street. I may be back.'

He was gone and once again there was a sigh of relief.

'You'll have plenty of time for fishing when we go on strike. Eh, Eamonn? Are there many queers in Ireland?'

Eamonn was reading the paper at this stage. The question

caused him to lower the paper and look out over the top at Albert.

'Are you telling me you've found female hormones in your body, Albert?'

'No. Eamonn. I'm not one.'

'Your friend, Malcolm, I'd say?'

'How did you know that, Eamonn?'

'I've great eyes. I could see the way he was looking over at you and laughing at you the other night in the Neptune.'

'You're right. He has a thing about me. What should I do?'

'It depends on what he wants. If it's a hand shandy – would you not give it to him?'

'Hand shandy?'

'I'm only kidding you, Albert.'

Anthony tipped Albert on the shoulder. 'Listen head, Skipper wants to see you at the counter.'

'Albert? I'm going over to see Larry in John of God's tonight. Will you come?'

'Yeah. I don't mind.'

'You can bring your girlfriend with you.'

'Eve's gone home. She's not coming back until tomorrow.'

'Bring your other girlfriend, Malcolm.'

'That's not funny Skipper. And you better leave me alone about him. I think I'm going to have to tell Malcolm to go and fuck off. I mean, the more I think about it, I hardly know him. Would you believe he was holding my hand on Saturday as we were walking home to the hostel?'

'As long as he wasn't holding your flute, you're alright. Listen, I'll see you later.'

*

The McEwan's siren sounded its five thirty signal. As Albert was putting on his duffle coat and leaving the office, he saw

159

Malcolm waiting for him. As he walked towards him Skipper passed.

'My girdle is killing me Malcolm. Where do you buy yours?'

Albert turned and walked away as Skipper spoke. Malcolm followed, and for a time they never said a word. The sound of the children could be heard from the flats as they played in the mild summer evenings.

'You told Skipper about me then?'

Malcolm had stopped. Albert did too.

'Look, Malcolm. I don't know what to say. Like, Eve is my girlfriend, and I want to get married to her and that's not going to ever change.'

Malcolm looked at him first and then turned. Albert noticed there was panic written on his face.

'Come on Malcolm? We'll go in for a drink.'

They went across to Gleeson's Pub and sat at the counter.

Malcolm reached his hand into his pocket and took out a watch. 'I bought you a watch. It's a Rolex. Please leave Eve for a while, come away with me, just until I sort myself out?'

'I don't want a watch, Malcolm. I don't want anything from you. I don't want to hurt or insult you. I just wish you would find some nice girl and things then will work out for you. Trust me? I know they will.'

'Eve's back now. Are you going to see her tonight?'

'The guard, Larry is in John of God's. Myself and Skipper are going over to see him, and afterwards I have to see Eve. Come with us to see Larry.'

160

30.

Skipper, Malcolm and Albert were in the waiting room as Larry Coyne emerged in his dressing gown.

'For fuck's sake, you've me all embarrassed over the play. Don't start giving out to me now over the lines. I've been a bit down lately, and I couldn't get a grasp of them.'

'It would be hard to embarrass you, Larry,' Skipper said. 'I didn't know you were one of those alcoholics?'

'Alcoholics me bollix. This is a haven of rest against the claws of the opposite sex. It's an excuse to say you're coming right and you're going to walk the straight and narrow. We have all these meetings and we play cards. It gets your thinking straight. You build up your credits again in the outside world. Sure when you get out you go even worse on the gargle. At least I find I always do. At least you get the certificate to say you're not well, and the Sergeant has to accept it whether he likes it or not. Fuck him, anyway. You always notice this place is always booked out after the Cheltenham Festival. Everybody's after losing their bollix, they go on a tear with the gargle till they come to terms with their loses and the wind of them has calmed down. Maybe we could put the play on in here, sure we could make it up as we go along? These people wouldn't know the difference.'

'I think we'll give the play a miss for a while. Can we bring you in anything?'

'Jaysis! Don't bring any gargle in here! You'll have me arrested.'

'Listen, we'll call in again and see you. Take care of yourself.'

'We're going down to see the girls.'

'More fucking drink. It's yous should be in here, not me.'

Larry walked them to the hall door and bid them goodnight.

31

Eve didn't need make-up, and Albert had never seen her wearing any until now. When Albert and Skipper walked into Grogan's Public House, Eve and Jill were sitting down waiting for them as arranged. Eve had a broad smile on her face as her eyes met Albert's. She was wearing the lightest of make-up, which only helped to highlight her fine features and her big brown glazed eyes. He could taste the sweet flavour of lipstick as she kissed him.

'Did you have a good time, Eve?'

'Fabulous. I missed you.'

'I missed you too.'

'Will I tell her or you, Albert?' Skipper said as he sat down.

'Tell me what, Albert?'

'Himself and Malcolm are thinking of eloping to Amsterdam. I'm sorry to disappoint you Eve, but they've fallen in love.'

Eve lifted her eyebrows and smiled at Albert. 'Don't mind him Albert. He's just jealous of how happy we are.'

Albert turned red with embarrassment. 'There's only one important person in my life, and that's you Eve. But there is something I have to tell you. Let me tell you later.'

'Can I stay with you tonight, Albert?'

'Of course. I'd love you to.'

'Hey Jill? You'll have to let me sleep with you tonight. I think you're getting sexier the older you get.'

'It's not that, Skipper. It's just you're such a super-stud.'

'Let's go and have an early night, Albert. You know what I

mean?' Eve revealed her pearl white teeth as she smiled. 'I'll get them a drink before we go. What will you have, Jill? Will I get you a pint, Skipper?'

'They're very soft and watery looking.'

'Will you have a large bottle of Guinness so?'

'You'll have a sore head in the morning after drinking large bottles.' Jill joined in.

'I wouldn't mind a sore head so much, but I don't want to have a sore hole after drinking watery pints. Listen, I just have to point Percy to the porcelain and we'll walk up the road with you.'

*

They say that absence makes the heart grow fonder, and despite the short duration of Eve and Albert's separation, they couldn't wait to get inside the flat for a bout of passionate love-making.

Albert held her in his arms as he spoke. 'We went to the Glen of Imall the weekend when you were away and Malcolm called me to one side. And you'll never guess what he told me.'

Eve gave a mischievous smile as she turned and looked into Albert's face. 'What's that, Albert?'

'Like this is embarrassing, Eve.'

'Tell me.'

'He said he was in love with me. I'm telling the truth.'

Eve burst into laughter.

'Is that funny? I mean this guy was serious. He put the shivers across me.'

'I'm not laughing at him, Albert. I'm laughing at you. You've been dying to tell me this.'

'It's just I didn't know what to say to him. I wanted to tell you, to see if you could offer me any advice. You're probably wondering what sort of weirdo I am, what with Dale and all that.'

'I know all about it, Albert.'

'I told you about Dale.'

'I know. What I mean to say is, I know all about Malcolm. He told me. He called to me before I went away.'

'What did he say?'

'He told me he'd kill me if I ever went near you again.'

Albert pulled away in shock. His heart was beating rapidly, and the blood rushed furiously to his face. He grinded his teeth. 'He said that?'

Eve put her arm around him and pulled him towards her with a smile on her face. 'Don't worry, Albert. Malcolm wouldn't hurt a fly. He's down, and when you're down you'll say anything. He's caught in a situation which he can't help, and when you're that vulnerable to depression, especially when you want something you can't have, you'd say or do anything. Especially when dealing with affairs of the heart. They hurt the most. If you want my advice, you'll try and help him sort it out by talking to him. Don't walk on him. That is the easiest thing to do when someone is down. My husband did it to me, and I had no one to turn to. And I thought his success would be my demise. Malcolm is on his own, like I was. You're different, you've got me. Now you see that strike is going to take place and you and me are going away together for a few months. Have a talk and be nice with him. You'd never know, someday you may be down yourself and you would be glad of the support of someone else. Come on Albert, go to sleep. You've to work in the morning.'

32

'Top of the morning, Albert.'

Eamonn was sitting opposite Albert.

'The more I think of it,' Eamonn said, 'the more I'm convinced I should have got a taxidermist.'

'Are you due some tax back, Eamonn?'

'No. I mean got him stuffed.'

Anthony was passing with a cup of coffee in his hand. 'Who, Mr Broderick? That would be impossible – sure he's already stuffed.'

'The salmon bass I caught in Mornington. If I got him stuffed in the first place he would be there on the mantelpiece as a shrine forever, for generations. No more proof would be required of my catch, of its size or weight. It could have been there for my future children to marvel at. Their father's great success story.'

'But sure you have a photograph of him? That's proof in itself.'

'It's not the same thing. I mean, take you looking at the photo. You said it was only fifteen inches. If a bird told me that I'd be mortified.'

Mr Broderick opened his door gently and walked like a penguin until he stood between Eamonn and Albert. It seemed to the workers that he had emerged from nowhere.

It was a strange coincidence considering Eamonn's subject matter, but today Mr Broderick really did look as though he had been stuffed.

'Wet time! Could ye be up to them? They don't deserve

work! I'll have to put the staff on protective notice, Eamonn! It will be only week to week, or perhaps day to day.'

His face was as round and white as a snowman's, and for a change he was holding his stomach in lieu of his balls. Only his lips moved as he spoke.

'Are you alright, Mr Broderick?' Eamonn enquired, giving Albert an ironic smile. 'I'd say you had a couple last night. Nothing wrong with that, seeing the auspicious times that's in it. A couple of alka-seltzers and you'll be as right as rain,'

'I have some here.' Anthony sprang from his chair like a frog being chased by a young boy.

A slight tremor darted through Mr Broderick. His eyes closed and his face creased as he inhaled the cigarette fumes from Anthony's mouth, making him look more foolish than nature had intended.

Anthony held out the enormous tablets.

'They're very big,' he declared. 'How many should I take?'

'Take about a dozen,' Anthony replied, a broad smile on his face.

'I think half a dozen will suffice,' Eamonn said evenly, fearing the worst.

He had as many hoisted into his mouth when one of the office girls brandished a glass. 'With water, Mr Broderick! With water.'

He picked up the glass with a robot-like motion and drank it. There was a stunned silence and Mr Broderick's head shook like Cassius Clay's punching bag during a training session. He let fly the gigantic roar of a prehistoric mammal and staggered on his way towards his den. He was but halfway there when a head gasket or stopcock burst open inside him, causing an explosive release of trapped air which was followed by the escape of the debris of his stomach itself.

All in the office held sombre expressions on their faces, determinedly looking towards the floor or picking up papers and pretending to have business elsewhere. Mr Broderick stood alone in the centre of the office. When the staff dared to look again, he had made an early exit.

Eamonn looked over at Albert. 'It looks like the strike has a ring of imminence for us. What will we do?'

'I'm going away to the country with Eve. I suppose you'll do some fishing?'

'I expect so.'

'Sure maybe you'll catch another Salmon bass as big as the last one and then you could get him stuffed.'

'It's seldom you get a second bite of the cherry.'

*

At five-thirty when Albert was leaving the office, he noticed Malcolm waiting outside.

An explosion of fury filled Albert's head. 'I want to see you, now!'

'Is something the matter Albert?'

'Yes Malcolm. Something really is the matter.'

They crossed the street and Albert stopped suddenly.

'What did you say to Eve?'

'Did she tell you I was talking to her?'

'Yes she did, because Eve tells me everything.'

There was a defenceless look on Malcolm's face, panic and searching tears in his eyes, the look of a man badly lost and looking for a home.

'I wouldn't hurt anyone Albert. If I did, it would only be myself.'

'If you even speak to her again, it won't be you killing her because I'll kill you. I don't ever want to see you again. Do you understand, Malcolm?'

'Please don't Albert... I don't know what I'll do if I can't see

168

you. I'm really miserable. Please don't say that?'

'Goodbye, Malcolm.'

Albert walked hurriedly away and watched a reflection of Malcolm in a shop window. Malcolm stood still with shock until Albert could not see him anymore.

*

As he approached his flat, Dale was waiting by the steps.

'Well, I'm glad to catch you Albert. I figured you'd be coming home from work around about now, so I decided to give you a shout. Now I know it's not Friday but you see I have to go away for a couple of weeks and I'll be sending someone else along to collect. His name is George Waters. I'm telling you so you won't be surprised when he makes himself known to you.'

'I wanted to see you.'

'Yeah. No problem, I hope.'

'We're going on strike in work, and I have to visit an aunt down the country that's not well. I wrote to her and told her I owed some money, so she sent me on some. So I wanted to pay you a number of weeks in advance.'

'You know Albert, I'm beginning to like you better by the day. I always knew I could trust you.'

'Will you wait here?'

'Sure Albert. Anything you say.'

Albert opened the latch on the door and hurried to get the money Eve had given him to pay Dale.

'That's twelve weeks in advance. You're a sound man Albert. And to show I appreciate your sincerity, I'm going to give you back a fiver. Let's call it friends' discount. I'm not that unreasonable a guy, and I promise you won't hear from me until after the twelve weeks. Have a good time and look after yourself. I'll even shake your hand. How's that?'

He pulled his collar up around his neck, shoved the money into his back pocket and walked around by Pembroke Street. Albert went to his room and sat on his bed, breathing a sigh of relief. It was nice to see the last of Dale, even if it was only for three months. He would enjoy a break in the country, especially with Eve. He put his hands behind his head as he lay on the bed. Had he been too cruel to Malcolm? He had done exactly the opposite of what Eve had asked him to do. He brought to mind the agonising look Malcolm had on his face when he departed from him. My God! What if Malcolm committed suicide? Would he ever be able to forget what he had said to him? I wouldn't hurt anyone Albert, Malcolm had said. If I did, it would only be myself.

His mind was returned to the present by the sound of his doorbell. Who could that be? Dale coming back looking for more money? Perhaps it was Malcolm. How should he treat him? He could not apologize to him, lest Malcolm might think his sexual preferences were now holding sway. The bell rang again. He got up and walked down the stairs. When he opened the door Jill was outside.

'How are you, Albert? Are you alone?'

'I'm surprised at seeing you? What brings you here?'

'Can I come up for a minute?'

'Yes. Of course. I'll make some tea.'

'Thanks.'

Jill sat on the sofa and started to laugh. 'Do you remember the first time I came in here? I'm sorry. I mean the first time you brought me in here?'

Albert turned away with embarrassment and poured the tea.

'Well, I was wondering if we could make-love again for old time sake?' Jill burst into laughter. 'I'm only joking you Albert. Skipper has me talking that way. He never gives over. No. I hadn't intended to call here at all. In fact, I was on my way over to see a friend that lives in Pembroke Lane when I saw you talking to someone at the door. I was wondering how you knew him.'

'Look Jill, I don't want any trouble.'

'Trouble?

'Yes, trouble. Myself and Eve are more than happy, and I want it to always be that way.'

'I'm serious. I was only joking about making-love. Dale Young, that's who it was. Wasn't it? Dale Young.'

'I have nothing to say about it, Jill.'

'How do you know him?'

'I don't.'

'And what did he want?'

'I can't say, Jill.'

'You can tell me Albert. He's my husband, you know. He's a creep. He's the one who got me into the street game. But I haven't lived with him for years. I wouldn't even speak to that shit.'

'He looks after you, you know what I mean? Before, for what you worked at. You and other girls doing the same thing.'

'Him? He couldn't look after himself.'

She stood up and narrowed her eyes as she walked towards Albert. 'What did he say to you? How does he know you? What did he want? Did he say something about me?'

'I can't say, Jill.'

'You can tell me, Albert. I'm your friend.'

'Can I? Are you sure there will be no trouble?'

'What's this all about?'

'Promise you won't get any of us in trouble.'

'Of course, I promise.'

'He told me you were one of his girls that he had on the game and I would have to pay him every week for using you or he would see there would be harm done to Skipper or you.'

Jill walked slowly backwards towards the couch. Her face had flushed. 'The fucking bastard!'

'He's been following us around ever since, even to the Glen of

Imaal. Are you saying he's not your pimp?'

'Him my pimp? He's a fucking shrimp! I have to go and get to the bottom of this. How long is this going on?'

'It must be six months. I think it all started in the Pembroke the first night you met Skipper. Do you remember the night Skipper got the black eye? You were there?'

'I remember. I didn't see what happened. I remember Skipper coming back to the seat with his eye cut. When I asked him what happened, he said he fell. But you mark my words, I will know what happened and I'll get that big ignorant slippery sneak.'

'Please Jill, he seemed so serious. I don't want any trouble.'

'Trouble? That waster couldn't punch his way out of a paper bag. That's what he is; a bag. A bag of bleedin' wind. Leave it with me Albert. I'll get your money back, don't you worry.'

She left. She had had a rude awakening. Albert believed she had known nothing about this. He could see that expression on her face, the expression of first knowledge. He sat back on the bed and felt relief that Jill was not the one crossing him. And besides, now she knew all about it. His mind switched as he thought of Malcolm. Maybe he should call over to him and see if he was alright?

*

At Malcolm's house, a cold shiver ran through Albert's spine when he learned that Malcolm had not yet returned from work. It was ten o'clock.

172

33

Skipper, Eamonn, Albert and Anthony were congregated around the counter outside the office. Skipper was glancing through the morning paper. Anthony had his cigarette upside down in the crook between his thumb and his index finger.

'Would any of you have known that, now?'

'What's that, Skipper?'

'Where does a woman have the curliest hair?'

'No doubt you're going to tell us Skipper,' said Eamonn, grinning.

'Of course. In Africa.'

The door opened and Mr Broderick stood still in the frame. The expression he wore on his face would have inspired a cartoonist.

'I think at lunch time we can bring the place to a close, Eamonn.'

'Och!' Anthony screamed and put his fingers in his mouth – startling Mr Broderick in the process and even causing him to remove his hand from his balls in fright.

'What was that in aid of, may I ask?'

Anthony did not answer, but stood as though frozen. The butt of his cigarette had become so small that it had burnt his fingers.

Mr Broderick eyes nearly popped out and he tightened his nose with a huge inhalation of polluted air. 'Lunch time so, Eamonn.'

'Let's say The Last Supper so, Mr Broderick.'

Mr Broderick did not answer, but turned and went back to his office.

Skipper called Albert aside. 'You should have told me Albert.'

'Jill told you about Dale?'

'Yes. I'll sort that out, don't worry. Myself and Jill went for a drink last night and Malcolm joined us.'

'Malcolm? Is he all right?'

'He looked a bit shocked. I didn't say anything to him that might upset him. We just talked about plays.'

'The phones are ringing!' Mr Broderick shouted from the main office.

'Well then answer them, you little fat bollix!' Skipper shouted back in a voice different to his own.

'Let's retire to the pub.'

'An excellent idea.'

The four men walked from the office out into the street. Albert glanced sideways as he passed the office window. Mr Broderick's face was nearly stuck to the glass in astonishment, his heavy breathing making the glass opaque.

34.

The sun emerged beyond the top of Ballinclea Mountain, casting a shadow into the Glen and making the mountain seem a hazy grey. The perfect blue sky illuminated the vastness of the universe. Yet the mountains of Lugnaquilla and Table were lit up by the rays of the sun. From where Eve and Albert stood they could see the purple heather and the brilliant yellow of furze.

The solid granite cottage was in a picturesque setting, just a short distance from the mountain. Eve and Albert excitably carried their belongings inside from the car which Eve's sister had lent them.

'Oh, Albert! Look at the open fireplace. And here, look out this window isn't the garden superb? Look at the hedges and the rich red of the escallonia! My God, Albert, it's heaven!'

They settled themselves into their new home, and then went walking through the meadows and across the Slaney towards the mountains. They walked hand in hand and sang in the desolate and lonely countryside, but felt far from lonely in this paradise. As the twilight set in, they returned to the cottage and lit a big fire from wood they had collected from the nearby forest.

'Come on, Albert. Let's pour some drink, and get nice and merry.'

'Yeah, why not.'

'Do you know the car my sister gave me a loan of? Do you know what make it is?'

'A Citreon.'

'Yes, that's right. She always wanted one of those. When she went to the garage, they had none in stock and she couldn't remember the type of car she wanted. The make. So she said it was like a Morris Minor with two sides cut square.' She took a sip of her wine. 'I forgot to ask you Ali, how did you get on talking to Malcolm or did you see him?'

'Yes. I saw him.'

'And is he okay?'

'Well, to tell you the truth I was very upset about what he had said to you and I told him so.'

'O Ali, you didn't upset him?'

Albert looked into Eve's worried eyes.

'It's causing me some bother,' he said, 'because I wasn't any help to him. In point of fact, I threatened him.'

'Never, Ali! It's not your nature.'

'I called around to apologise. But he wasn't there. He hadn't been home from the time I spoke to him earlier.'

'O God, Ali! I can't believe it! I'll not rest till I find out that he is okay. Write to him, explain, please! Sometimes it's easier to explain in a letter than having to try and explain face to face. Come on, Ali. Get another drink and we'll compose a letter now.'

They stayed up until three in the morning doing just that, along with laughing and drinking.

*

And they spent weeks in heavenly bliss at the cottage; most days walking up over the mountains and surveying the countryside. On many evenings, they swam nude in the Slaney river which ran through the back of the cottage. Afterwards, they often sat on the bank and talked for hours on end about anything and everything. Sometimes Eve would sit out the back of the cottage, looking at the mountains, trees, the lilac flowers and the river, painting. Sometimes they fished for hours and brought home fresh trout.

'Just looking at that small trout there brings Eamonn to mind.'

'That's not a small fish.'

'It is in relation to the one Eamonn caught in Mornington. His was seventeen and a half inches. He claims he should have got him stuffed to stake his claim to fame. He's the tall good-looking man with black hair. Although it was only one of his claims to fame.'

'What was the other?'

'He was taught in school by Paddy Crosbie. He came in to work a few times to buy some timber, and Eamonn introduced me to him. He's a radio star. He does a programme called 'The School around the corner'. He seemed a nice enough man. He had a very distinctive voice; spoke through his nose.'

And they would talk and laugh and make love as often as the day was long.

*

Their holiday was in its third week. A morning came when they had planned a pleasant walk over the mountain. Eve turned to Albert as they lay in bed.

'Would you think me a spoilsport if I didn't go today Ali? I'm sorry. I don't feel up to it. I'd just like to sit in the garden.'

Albert looked into her eyes and could see she was crying. 'We don't have to go anywhere, Eve. You're not ill, are you?'

'I don't want you to get worried or anything Ali, but I'm pregnant.'

'Pregnant? Are you sure?'

'Yes. I didn't want to spoil our holiday, but I haven't been well lately. I've been getting sick, mostly at night. They call it morning sickness.'

'Oh! You poor thing! You should have told me! And me

177

dragging you up all those mountains!'

He looked into her glazed eyes and smiled, offering her some comfort. 'Really, Eve? You mean you're pregnant? My God, our own child... I'm going to be a father.'

'You mean you're really glad, Albert?'

'God, I can't believe it! I'm delighted! That's the best news I've ever heard! You just stay here in bed and I'll bring you your breakfast, and then we'll drive into Baltinglass and go and see a doctor. I'm sure he can give you some tablets to make you feel better.'

'Oh Ali, you're something else.' She smiled. 'Come here, I feel better already. And I've something else to tell you.'

'Don't tell me anymore until I get your breakfast. Wait till I open the curtains. There! Look Eve. The sun is flowing from the heavens!'

He was delirious with excitement, and busied himself around the kitchen getting the breakfast. Afterwards, they went out in the car to the doctor.

'Look at the scenery Ali, isn't it breathtaking? See there, the farmer harvesting the rye crop. Albert I have to tell you, I always wanted a child of my own. I didn't plan it that way because I thought I couldn't have children. A doctor down the country told me once he didn't think I could have any children. I suppose when I got married to someone who had a child, I thought it would be a ready made home. I really got on very well with his daughter, Jessica. We walked together and talked together, and I really loved her. I suppose it's nice to have something special to remember in a marriage; and for me she was it. But now all has changed since I met you, something special that I thought never would or never could happen to me. Life has a way of acting strangely; we never know what's around the corner! Right now, I can't believe we're having our own child.' In her enthusiasm, she took his hand.

'Hey Eve?' Albert laughed. 'Take it easy. The car is wobbling on the road. Keep your two hands on the wheel. It would just be our luck to hit a tree and both be killed.'

'Don't say that Ali!'

*

'I don't know. I'll give you this prescription. See if it makes you feel any better. What brings you out this neck of the woods?'

'Well, we're on a kind of a holiday. A long holiday. A few months actually, Doctor.'

'Well, if you're getting sick that often it would be as well to cut it short and pay a visit to the hospital. Try these antibiotics, and should there be no improvement, then it's definitely to the hospital.'

'Thanks Doctor.'

They drove to the chemist, got the tablets and went back to the cottage.

'Albert? Do you know what I'm going to do? I'm going to ask James to give us a hand buying this cottage. I know we could get it cheap, and then we could open a painting and pottery shop. Sell all sorts of odds and ends. Would you like that?'

'Absolutely brilliant, Eve.'

Albert brought a deckchair down to the Slaney River, and some sandwiches. Eve had a book in her hand while Albert fished for trout.

'I'm going up to the cottage for a while, Ali. You stay fishing, here. I'll come back in a while.'

'Are you sure you're okay? Do you want me to come up with you, Eve?'

'No, I'm alright.'

'Are those tablets making you feel better?'

'I think so. I'll catch you in a while.'

Albert continued fishing, until he realised that Eve was gone for some considerable time. He laid his rod by the bank and walked up to the cottage.

'Eve?' The kitchen was deserted.

'I'm in here Albert, in the bedroom.'

'Are you al right, Eve?'

'God, Albert. I can't believe it. I'm really sick.'

'What can I do, Eve?'

Eve was crying and was in a cold sweat. 'I don't know. I've been puking up blood. I'm losing the child.'

'Can you drive?'

'I don't think so, Ali. I've no strength. I just don't know.'

'Can you wait here just for a half an hour? I'll get that old pushbike that's in the shed and call down to Fentons. Will you wait here?'

She nodded.

*

Albert rushed out to the outhouse, grabbed the old pushbike and hurried to the Glen.

'Mrs Fenton?' he said as he rushed into the bar.

'Are you alright, Albert?'

'It' Eve, Mrs Fenton. She seems so sick. We went to the doctor today, and he said if she wasn't any better, she would have to go to James' Hospital. She has a car but I can't drive.'

'George? Get the car.'

*

George drove through Blessington as fast as he could. By the time they hit Brittas, they had to stop and let Eve out for she got sick again. She had her hand to her mouth and couldn't speak a word.

180

'I'll pull in at the Garda Station in Tallaght, Albert. The guards can call an ambulance.'

They were helping her out of the car when a guard came to help. The guard put a blanket around her and they sat her down while another called an ambulance. The sound of the siren could be heard from the distance, and then Eve and Albert were in the back holding hands as it tore through the city. Eve lay down as though dead and Albert was shivering.

Her stretcher was brought out with speed when they arrived at the hospital.

The nurse greeted Albert. 'Don't worry, child. She's in good hands. Would you wait here in the waiting room please? What happened to her?'

'I don't know, nurse. She's pregnant.'

'Are you a relation of hers?'

'No – I'm mean yes. I'm her boyfriend. I mean, we're going to get married.'

'Don't worry. She'll be fine. I'll get you a cup of tea. Just wait here and you'll see I'm right. The doctor is with her and he'll confirm exactly what I've told you.'

*

He sat there for half an hour with bated breath, sipping tea until the doctor came out.

'Are you Albert Cagney? She's been asking about you. You can go in and see her. She will have to stay here until we do some tests and an X-ray. Go in for a while and then let her rest. Tomorrow we'll let you know how she is.'

'What's wrong, Albert? What's happening to me?'

'I don't know, Eve. They're going to do some tests and we'll know tomorrow. You have to stay here tonight. How do you feel?'

'Better, Ali. A lot better.'

'Now, there you are,' said the nurse as she entered the room. 'I told you she was fine. Now why don't you leave and let her have some rest, and come back to us tomorrow? Eve will be alright.'

'Where will you stay tonight, Ali?'

'In the flat in Leeson Street. Take care of yourself Eve, and I'll come and see you tomorrow. I love you.'

'And I love you too, Ali.'

*

When he left the hospital, Albert called to Davey and Sinéad but they were not in. He went home and went to bed, but could not sleep for sleep had abandoned him. His room was cold and ghostly compared to the picturesque setting were he had lived with Eve.

*

Davey and Sinead were shocked when they heard the news the next morning. All three made their way to the hospital.

'She is in with the surgeon and the doctor at present.' The nurse directed them to a waiting room.

'What's the matter with her?' Sinéad asked. 'They're not operating on her? Or are they?'

'No. They're just establishing what exactly's the problem. Why don't you wait in the waiting room and I'll tell you when they're finished.'

*

'Hello. My name is Mr Matthews. I am one of the hospital's surgeons. You are relatives of Miss Robertson?'

'I'm her brother, David. We're orphans. But this is Sinéad – her family adopted her. And this is her boyfriend, Albert.'

'Would you be kind enough to follow me to my office, please?'

'Nothing has happened to her?' Albert asked.'

'No.'

'Did she lose her baby?'

The surgeon led them to his office, and invited them to sit down.

'I know she did!' said Albert. 'She lost the baby!'

'Eve is not pregnant. She was of the opinion that she was, but I'm afraid what I have to say is not good news.'

'She's okay, isn't she?' said Albert.

'We have just completed an examination on Eve, and a number of X-rays. It is with great regret that we have discovered a tumour above her left breast, beside her left shoulder. We are not one-hundred percent sure, but we feel it is quite likely that it's malignant. We have not told her as yet as we awaited your advice. It would be essential we get a biopsy to establish how serious it is; but we feel certain it's serious.'

Albert was shivering. 'What does this mean, Doctor?'

'Well, as I said it's extremely dangerous. There are only two options. The first is that we try a radiation course if it proves to be malignant, which we're pretty sure it is. On the other hand: we could try and remove the tumour, which is large, and would most likely mean her losing her arm.'

Albert ran out to the toilet and got sick.

The nurse met him as he was leaving. She put her arm around his shoulder in an effort to comfort him, but his tears kept coming.

'Come on, child. You want to see her, don't you? You wouldn't like to upset her by letting her see you cry. Here, take this tissue and wipe those tears away. Now, let me get you a cup of tea and then we'll go in and see her. Things are not always as bad as they seem.'

Sinéad and Davey were already in the ward when Albert entered. Eve was almost sitting because of the backrest support.

183

She put out her hand as Albert sat on the bed.

'Well, Albert? Have you missed me already?'

He could not look at her for his eyes were scorched.

'There you are now Eve. He has had no sleep,' said the nurse. 'He has been up all night worrying about you. The Surgeon would like to see you, Eve. After all those tests, I think you could do with a good sleep as well. Why not all come back tomorrow and you'll all be nice and fresh for a long chat?'

As they left, the nurse pulled a screen around her and the surgeon entered.

*

They walked down Thomas Street. Not a lot of words were spoken for there were not a lot of words to be said.

'The surgeon suggested that he tell Eve the situation for better or worse,' Sinéad said. 'He felt there was no point keeping her in the dark. So we told him he could. I'll have to ring my Mam and Dad,'

'I'm going to call over to Skipper and get pissed drunk!' said Albert.

'No Albert. That's not going to prove anything,' said Davey. 'It will only make you feel worse later.'

'I'll see you tomorrow.'

'Don't give up hope Albert,' Davey said as they parted. 'I haven't.'

*

Skipper answered the door and invited Albert in. 'What are you doing here? I thought you were in the Glen. Donie and myself were just going down there tomorrow. Listen, I've talked to Jill and we've given Dale some thought. We've got to get him down to

184

the Glen and iron out the differences.' Skipper stopped. 'What wrong with you? Your eyes are all bloodshot!'

'Eve's in hospital, Skipper.'

'Yeah? Nothing serious I hope?'

'She's got a tumour.'

'Cancer? Come on in here, Albert. Trassie, it's Albert.'

'You're welcome, Albert. God now, I haven't seen you since the play. Skipper, get Albert a bottle of stout. And how are you keeping?'

'I can't believe what I've heard, Trassie,' said Skipper. 'Don't you know Eve, the girl who was playing Mary in the play? She's Albert's girlfriend. Albert has just told me she's in hospital.'

'That's the real pretty looking lass with the dark hair and the brown eyes.'

'Will you have one Trassie?'

'I will, Skipper.'

'I've just been to see the surgeon and he told me she has a tumour beside her arm.'

'God help us,' Trassie said.

Albert started to cry. 'The doctor said it was very serious and she could lose an arm.'

Trassie looked up at Skipper as she wheeled her way over towards Albert. 'Doctors aren't always right. What about Paddy Farrell, Skipper? It must be fifteen years

since I was told he had cancer. I know I was only a child. Now I've never seen him looking better. Amn't I right, Skipper?'

'He'd drink the two of us under the table.'

'I can see you're very upset, child. The poor girl.'

'Albert, lives on his own in a flat in Leeson Street,' said Skipper. 'They had just gone on a long holiday to the Glen of Imaal.'

'Let him stay here with us Skipper, until everything settled down. Will we go down to the pub? Will you bring me?'

'I will, Trassie. Wait 'til I shave myself.'

35.

Albert walked into the ward, alone, and Eve flung her arms around him.

She broke into hysterics. 'Jesus Christ, Albert – I don't believe it! – I don't want to fucking die! Take me out of here. Don't let them take me before the sand passes the quarter! Take me out of here, Albert.'

They held one another, crying, until the nurse came into the ward.

'We want to get out of here nurse,' said Albert. 'We're going home. Would you get me her clothes?'

'Just hold on a minute.'

The nurse left the ward, and returned with a doctor.

He tried to give them a heartening smile. 'So you want to go home? Yes Eve, you can if you feel up to it. But it might be better if you stayed another night.'

'Your Mam and Dad are coming up from the country today and they're on their way in to see you,' said the nurse. 'They want to talk to us so that they can do the best for you. I had them on the phone.'

Eve looked up to Albert. 'Am I going to be okay, Doctor?'

'We're going to do everything we can for you.'

'We'll be at your beck and call night and day Eve,' said the nurse.

'Well, I'll wait and see Mam and Dad and go home tomorrow. I have some clothes in your flat, Ali. Will you bring them in?'

'Of course I will.'

'Will you come and see me this evening?'

'I will. But maybe your Mam and Dad would like to have time with you alone? They don't often see you, and they'll have driven a long way?'

'Right.'

'I'll come tomorrow.'

'Give me a kiss Ali.'

The nurse and the doctor turned away to allow them the comfort of each other. He leaned over the bed and kissed her, and they spent a long time saying goodbye.

*

'Eve wants to come home, Trassie. I've got to bring her clothes. So, thanks for putting me up. I'll have to go home tomorrow and get the flat ready. I'll have to look after her 'til she feels better.'

Skipper passed them a bottle of stout each and sat beside them. He glanced up to Trassie. 'What did the Doctor say?'

'Oh,' said Albert. 'He said she could come home.'

'You know Albert, I don't want to dictate to you,' Trassie said, 'but you've got to be strong during these times, because her seeing your strength may give her strength. You've got to encourage her to want to get better. I've been through it and I know, because I got the support I needed from the man sitting beside you.'

'Here!' said Skipper. 'Get the violins and the hankies out! Speaking of out, I think it's out we'll go for our liquid dinner. Do you want to come with us, Trassie?'

'No, you two go ahead. I'll have a couple of bottles of stout here with your uncle Tommy who's coming over to see me. Where are you going?'

'We'll go for a bit of a walk so; up around Stephen's Green.

We'll probably go into Mc Daid's for a couple.'

'There's a bit of stew in the pot for when you come back. You don't go eating those old greasy chips!'

*

'Your good health, gentlemen. I called upstairs to your abode because you were conspicuous in your absence, young Albert.'

'How are you Peter?'

Albert's neighbour was sitting at the counter as they went into McDaid's.

'I'm anything but well, financially speaking. Much to my detriment, I was toying with the glorious uncertainties of the turf.'

'I'd say you'd miss Larry with his tips?' Albert said.

'That wouldn't be altogether true. Save for that winner that day, he has endowed me with a lot of good things that when tested have found to be waiting for more marrow on their bones.'

'I can give you a tenner, Peter,' Skipper said, 'Were you in to see Larry?'

'I see you're heavily in leaf. I should think that will fall high on my appreciation list. Alas, I wasn't in to see the man who keeps our city under control. I must admit I'd be reluctant to bother even the perimeter of that establishment, lest they clamp eyes on me. For if they did I would imagine it would be some time before they'd let me out.'

The door opened and Malcolm walked in, but having observed Albert he retraced his steps and made haste through the exit.

Albert ran out after him. 'Malcolm! Malcolm!'

Malcolm stopped in his stride, but did not look around.

Albert caught up on him. 'Malcolm. I was worried about you. How have you been?'

'You have a peculiar way of showing your worry; and I've been sick if you must know.'

189

'Look Malcolm, but it wasn't my intention to hurt you. Did you get my letter?'

'No. I got a letter alright – but it was written by Eve. It was intelligently planned, because it said exactly what Eve already had told me.'

'I'm sorry. I really am. Eve is very ill, and I'm really on a low.'

'I'm sorry to hear about Eve. But I'm not sorry about you, that you're down. I seem to remember asking your help and you refused. You see, those that don't give help shouldn't expect any in return.'

'Yeah, well maybe you're right.'

He had smartened himself up so that he looked as he had when Albert first met him, and he looked more assertive and in control of himself. Albert looked into his eyes as he looked into his. He put out his hand for Malcolm to shake. Malcolm looked at it for an instant and then walked away.

*

Eve was lying on the bed smiling as he entered the ward. He was taken aback by how well she looked.

'How are you, Eve?'

'I'm great, I feel great. It's good to see you.'

'Yeah, well it's great to see you too. I brought your clothes.'

'Mam and Dad were here all day yesterday, and I told them about the wonderful time we were having. About the rivers, the flowers, the sunsets and the mountains. And of course our lovely cottage. And James told me to get well and he'd buy it for us. Isn't that sweet? Just the two of us together. Be best friends and grow old together.' She put her hand to her face and gave her girlish giggle. 'I was in so much pain that the doctor gave me this injection, morphine it was, and I haven't stopped talking since. My God, Albert it's bigger than pot. We decided that it's best I stay

190

here and undergo radiation treatment. I have to go for half an hour each day. I hope you're not disappointed I'm not going home. They look after me better here.'

'All I want is for you to get better.'

'Yes. When you lie here everything comes back to you. All the wrongs you've done, and all the things you want to do right in the future. I've stayed awake all night thinking of the years I wasted with my husband. Ali, let's not have the wallpaper and the curtains matching in our cottage. Let's not be always cleaning and tidying and dusting. And let's always talk and be best friends.'

'Did he not talk with you?'

'He didn't know how to talk, he screamed all the time. This wasn't in the right place, that wasn't in the right place. He had to work to get this, he had to work to get that. He had no sense of humour. He only laughed when he learned of someone's downfall.'

'How come you married him?'

'I was young and in love. Jesus, he told me I never grew up. I opened this little boutique to get away from the house. I got into debt with rent, and he went berserk. He was obsessed with money. He would come home from the hospital and tell me how hard he had to work and how little I had done to the house while he was away. His presence in the house and the way he ran around screaming was a constant reminder of my failures. So I used to go out and walk and go into the pub where I got some good comfort from friends. Then he starts telling people I was an alcoholic. Putting grotesque labels on me. Why are people so cruel, Ali? Where do they learn to hate?'

'I don't know, Eve.'

'I should have copped on, because he had an uncle and an aunt that his family had also labelled as alcoholics. They wouldn't even invite them to our wedding. I met them, and Jesus they were a hundred percent sounder than he was. The aunt now is looking after the rest of them in their old age.'

Albert started to laugh.

'Wait till I tell you, Ali. The men down in his hometown rattle the cup off the saucer when they want more tea. I'm serious.'

'Where do the come from, Eve?'

'Wicklow town.'

'What did O' Casey say in Juno and the Paycock? A Wicklow Man. Oh ,that explains it.'

'One day he told me he was studying pharmacology, and I asked him was he sorry I wasn't more farm-orientated. And would you believe, he went around telling everybody I thought pharmacology was to do with farming. I'm talking too much Ali, amn't I?'

'You're not, Eve. I'm enjoying you. You never told me before about him.'

'No I didn't. He wasn't an interesting enough a person to talk about, except when you're drugged.'

'How did you split up?'

'He took me to court, put me on the dock. Spent a fortune on it.'

'Are you sorry? Do you hate him?'

'No, Ali. I don't hate him. I'm not made of that kind of metal, no more than yourself. But I fear for him; the harm he may cause others.'

*

A long number of weeks passed as Eve underwent radiation, but the reports given to her family were still negative

As the days passed and the treatment went on she grew weaker and weaker. Eventually, the surgeon wanted to take her aside for three days without anyone visiting her to allow her to recover from the effects of the radiation.

Albert called as soon as he was allowed in to see her. He could not believe his eyes, for she was more like a little child lying in the bed. He tried hard to hold back his tears.

'Ali. I don't think I'm getting better. I got the nurse to put make-up and lipstick on me before you came. Do I look okay?'

'Yes Eve, you do.'

'Come in beside me Ali and mind me. Just for a while.'

'Yes.'

'Should anything happen to me Ali, I want you to meet a nice girl, someone who'll be your best friend. Make sure she is during you downs as well as you ups and you'll never have a serious problem.'

'I don't want anybody but you, Eve. I don't want anyone but you.'

36

The surgeon called all her family to his office and told them that she would only survive for a matter of days or hours.

'And is there a chance at all she could live?' James asked through a choking throat. 'Even a miracle?'

'Not that we can envisage happening. I'm sorry, Mr and Mrs Robertson.

*

All her friends were gathered around in the hospital ward. She could scarcely see them and her voice was barely audible. She spoke slowly. 'Why is everyone here? Albert? Does this mean my time is at an end?'

Only Skipper had enough strength to walk towards her. 'They're just your family and your friends, Eve. They've come to see you.'

The others glanced at her or stood with their eyes on the floor.

'Is Albert here, Skipper?'

'I am, Eve.'

'Do you remember the first evening I met you?'

He had no control over his tears or voice. Eve's lips were broken and dry, and Skipper put his hand to her back and lifted her forward to place a glass of water to her lips.

'Yes, Eve, I remember,' Albert said.

'Do you remember the song I sang?'

'I do.'

'What was it, Albert?'

'Sweet Carnlough Bay.'

She tried to hum it for a moment, but couldn't. Skipper reached and gave her some water.

'And what was the song you sang, Albert?'

'I can't remember.'

'I can, Ali. It was 'The Parting Glass'.'

Her eyes closed for a moment as her body jolted suddenly in pain. 'You know, Dad and Mam and all my friends, I'm glad you all came, for the pain doesn't seem to hurt anymore. I'm not afraid now that you're all here. Ali? Take my hand, and please look at me always. I'm not bad to look at now, am I?'

'You're the sweetest looking girl in the world Eve,' her father said and he moved closer towards her.

'Take my hand Ali, and sing it for me, 'The Parting Glass'. You know the first verse; it's my epitaph.'

'I... can't.' He backed towards the exit door and ran out down the hall way to the little church.

He knelt down and looked up at the crucifix of the Lord. The only other person in the church was a nun. She looked over at him and smiled. He stared at the crucifix in deep thought and swore that he would never again ask for a favour in his life if the good Lord would make her better. He spoke deeply in his own words from his heart, and got up and went back to the ward.

Everyone stared at him as he walked back into the room, and his eyes lit up as he entered. His heart heaved as he took her by the hand. It seemed the good Lord had answered his prayers.

The door opened again a moment later and her husband entered. He walked slowly towards her, extending his hand; but she would not take it, and she turned away from him and tried to whisper something to Albert.

*

And the Lord did answer his prayers, though not in the way Albert hoped. He answered them in a way that someday we humans may understand; by asking his angels to sound triumphant horns, and to go on their mission to earth and carry her soul back through those clouds she much loved so He could welcome her to His kingdom.

Just before the angels had done so, Eve's friend's and family noted what was happening and they turned away. She closed her eyes for her final sleep. Albert stood unable to grant her final request or even to look at her, for he was so torn with hurt.

At the end, Skipper offered her some comfort by holding her hand and his composure; though even he was grinding his teeth, for all the steel he was made of.

37

The guard, Larry Coyne, sat at the centre of the counter in Fenton's pub. He was in a paralytic state and had four full pints in front of him. He was giving them escort duty while pondering how he could make room for the same. He was puffing like the wolf in the story of the three pigs. With effort, he lifted his right leg just enough to relieve his posterior of offensive gases.

'Ah, you're after opening your lunch again, Larry. Give us a break, for fuck's sake. This is only a small room.'

'If you were caught in a hole, you'd be glad to get out of it.'

Skipper, Jill, Albert, Anthony and Eamonn were up at the dartboard, playing darts. Despite this, there was suspense in the air and the atmosphere was more subdued than usual. Mrs Fenton had detected the tension, and she panned her eyes around looking for the cause.

The guard picked up another pint and his body tightened as the door opened. He looked through the reflection in the mirror. Yes. It was Dale with three rough looking men. Skipper saw him, but turned away as though nothing unusual was about to happen. A silence fell around the bar, and then calmly the Professor spoke loudly. 'I say, is that him? Is that the one you've been waiting for?'

Skipper looked down the bar and caught Dale straight in the eye. They stared at one another for a time, neither wilting, until Dale started to walk towards Skipper. Jill looked at Dale. She had scorn written all over her face, and her hand rested on Skipper's shoulder. Dale was stopped halfway when the guard stood up with great effort from the stool, blocking Dale's path.

'I want to fucking see you outside.'

'And who the fuck are you suppose to be?' said Dale. 'You big fat bollix, get out of my way.'

'Here now,' Mrs Fenton said, 'we'll have no trouble here. I have the Guards here in five minutes'

'They're here,' said Larry. 'Who the fuck do you think I am, ma'am? Give our friends here a drink, and then I want to see you outside.'

Dale looked up at Skipper, and then turned towards the bar. Everyone got up and walked out of the bar with the exception of Mrs Fenton, Dale and his three friends.

They gathered in the square outside the pub. Larry stood outside, swaying to and fro and looking at the exit door. Albert's heart jumped as the door opened and Dale and his cohorts emerged. He could sense the potent feelings of menace between Skipper and Dale. Dale walked through the crowd which split in two to make a path for him.

'Now hold it,' said Larry. 'I have a few important things to say. I'm a guard now, don't forget that. But first, I have to draw water. I'm bursting.'

'Well Jill?' said Dale. 'How are you keeping?'

'None the better for seeing you, you prick.'

Dale forced a smile and looked back at his friends. There was a roar of motorbikes. Dale nodded and advanced further. The motorbikes pulled in, five in all, and a weird-looking crew got off them to join Dale's friends. Albert heart was beating hard as he looked over at the bikers. Some wore helmets with leather jackets and jeans. Their hair was greased and some of them wore sunglasses.

'I believe you asked me out here to see you?' said Dale. 'Well I'm here.'

'Well, you know, I figure you owe my friend here some money. I mean a lot of money. And I'm looking for it back.'

'And you're going to do something about it?'

Skipper had not anticipated that Dale would have such a following. It caused him some concern, but since things had reached this stage he could not wilt.

Larry Coyne appeared at the pub door. He had a half pint in his hand which he put on the windowsill while he closed the fly of his trousers. He began shouting at the top of his voice as he staggered towards them. He wedged himself between Skipper and Dale, pushing them apart with his hands. 'Now, for fuck's sake listen to me. Yous want to have it out. Yis have your differences. Well now, I'm going to referee. Now I'm not wearing me uniform, but if I have to use my powers I'll use them. Yous better strip off to the waist, because this will only be man to man. It will be Queensbury rules. There'll be no dirt. Do yis understand me?'

At this point, he was hanging onto their lapels; in fact they were holding him up.

'I have a whistle here,' he continued, 'and when I blow you'll start; and when I blow again, yis'll stop. Do yis fucking understand me?' And if there's any dirt from anyone, I'll personally book them and beat the bollix out of them meself. Get us a chair, I'm fucked. And pass me over me pint. Now, get ready. Right?'

'That seems fair enough,' said one of the bikers.

Jill gave Skipper a hand off with his shirt. Albert went to get a chair for the guard. The two men stood eight feet apart and stared at one another. Dale went to release the buckle on his belt.

'I'm watching. I'm fucking watching. I said Queensbury rules. Do yous hear me?' The crowd formed a ring around Dale and Skipper. Larry brought the whistle to his mouth and blew.

The two men circled around each. They had their fists held up for the encounter, and each watched the other like a hunter watches prey. Skipper lunged forward and took Dale by surprise.

199

He pulled his right leg back in flight and released it as if from a catapult sling, depositing his climbing boot right between the arch of Dale's trousers. Dale lowered his hands to his testicles, crumbling to the ground in horrendous pain with his face turning purple.

By reflex, the guard also cupped his testicles imagining what the pain was like. 'Right,' he said. 'That's fair enough. It's over now. Come on, somebody has to buy me a gargle.'

One of Dale's friends walked forward towards the guard. 'What do you mean, that's fair enough? You said it had to be a fair fight. Queensbury rules, remember?'

'Well, it was fair. The way that fucker plays. I saw him going for his buckle belt.'

'Hold on a minute, pal!'

The five bikers moved forward, removing their helmets while in transit.

'By Jaysis! Look who it is. It's Larry. What's the story, Larry?'

'How are you Einstein? Come on in. Bring your mates in, and I'll explain what it's all about over a jar.'

They walked into Fenton's Pub and Larry sat beside Terry and explained all about Dale and Albert and the money he had paid.

Terry left the pub and went out to Dale and his three friends. After a time he returned and approached Albert.

'I want to buy you a drink, pal. I heard about your problem with your girlfriend. Larry told me. Here's your money returned; he won't bother you again if he knows what's good for him.'

'Thanks Terry.'

'No need to mention it. You know I found out what Einstein's theory on relativity was. It's to do with the interconnection of time and space.'

38.

'Time heals all wounds', we're told. It would take some time for Albert's heart to heal. He would have to try and put the tragedy behind him and get on with his life, however bleak the future seemed without his greatest companion. She would never leave his mind, and his weekly visits to her graveyard made him think constantly of how beautiful a creature she was. And yet however perfect Eve had been, the good Lord had decided to take away.

It was a visit some seventeen months later that the Christmas winter sent large snowflakes floating from the sky, and the lonely despondent graveyard was a white carpet of death. He could see no one in sight, and he spoke in scarcely audible whispers as he placed a shrub of lilacs on the grave. He had brought it all the way from the cottage where they stayed.

'I know you always liked them, their colour. You told me yourself; they had that special pink colour, or that violet you saw in the mountains for the first time in the distance. I have those colours hanging up in that last painting you did outside that cottage in the Glen. Everything is so quiet now. I spend most of my time alone, reading those plays and poems that we talked about so much during our wonderful holiday. Even Skipper has left the scene. I heard himself and Jill parted company; and I hear that he too spends most of the time alone, or at least with his sister, who is such a nice person. I haven't forgotten, Eve, today is your birthday. You're getting old; you're all of twenty six. And by coincidence, I have an audition with the abbey theatre today, on your birthday. I know you'd be proud for me and wish me well. I've prepared a piece from Ckekhov, and of course our O'Casey. It's almost Christmas. I know you'll have a happy time where you are, and I promise I'll keep myself straight; and the day will come when we'll be together again. I'll be back to see you after Christmas.'

39

Albert did not get the part in the Abbey. When he reached the door of his flat he decided not to go in but to take a walk up by the canal. As he walked along the banks between the locks, he saw a guard standing on the opposite side of the street who called him by his name. It was Larry Coyne. He smiled over at him and then crossed the road.

'For fuck's sake Albert, how are you keeping? I haven't seen you for years. You know, that's some bollix of a Sergeant. I had all this gear on, the cape and all, and he put me on duty in the Dáil. The central heating was burning the place, and I was sweating like a pig having a ride in a sauna. It's just as well he changed me in the evening, otherwise they would be taking me out in a coffin. I'm only after been talking to Jill. She's back serving the public with the oldest profession. Skipper must have got tired of the furry bun-burger, although he used to say it was the best craic he ever had without smiling.'

'Did you give up the drink, Larry?'

'I did in me bollix. Sure I hung around with drinkers and gamblers all me life, and I have to say they were the soundest bunch you'd ever meet. I know everyone says they talk the world of shit; but if they are shit, you don't be long about knowing it. You know what a drunkard is thinking, but you don't know what a person who doesn't drink is thinking. I've seen more poets and writers and actors looking to drink to give them relief from the person they wanted to be. Do you remember Einstein, Terry, the bin man? You wouldn't believe him if you saw him. He gave up that rough game, and goes to night school, Dalton's, up in Rathmines. You'd want to be an intellectual to talk to him now.'

'It's good to see. I'll move, now.'

'Yeah. Take care of yourself. Jill was just around the corner. Why don't you give her a shout? I sure she'd do you a turn.'

'I see you around, Larry.'

'Hey Albert? Before you go, I know it was very sad about Eve, but do you remember just before she died she whispered something to you? What was it she said?'

'She just said I love you, I always will. See you Larry.'

'Yeah. Look after yourself, son. There will be better times ahead.'

Albert walked on. Children had made a huge slide, and were playing and laughing on the side of the road. He stood and watched them for a time, before walking on towards Fitzwilliam Place.

She smiled as he approached her. She was blowing her hands through her gloves to try and keep out the cold.

'It's been a long time, Albert. Are you well?'

'I'm fine, Jill. And you?'

'Great. As you can see, it's hard to kick off old habits. The money is too good. I think it was in this very place I first met you. A few years ago, right?'

'Yeah. It seems a long time ago.'

'You look great.'

'You too, Jill.'

'Did you hear Dale had to do a runner out of the country? You won't see him back here again. Listen Albert, I'm frozen and business is poor. Why don't we go back to your place for a cup of coffee? That's if you don't mind?'

'Yeah. It would be nice to have someone to talk to for a change.'

He put his arm around her shoulder, and they walked through the deep snow. Leeson Street was a white sheet of desolation, except for the street light which added to the softness with its lantern yellow lights. The sound of a party in a house could be heard. It was the raw-edged voice of Dylan singing, 'how does it feel to be on your own, like a rolling stone'. His voice signalled a time of change.

'Poor Eve. Albert, do you miss her a lot?'

'Very much.'

'What was the song she wanted you to sing that she said was her epitaph? You didn't sing it for her?'

'No.' He began to sing softly as they walked.

Oh, of all the money e'er I spent,

I spent it in good company,

And of all the harm that e'er I've done,

Alas it was to none but me.

And all I've done for want of wit,

To memory now I can't recall.

So fill for me the parting glass,

Goodnight and peace be with you all.

'Gosh, Albert. Can you believe, it will be Christmas in two days.'